'I think they're out to destroy E-15,' Peppiatt said. 'We'll have to defend, you know, professor. Lots of lives at stake.'

The 'copter landed near the adjustor and the pilot got out and spoke to Haldane, the chief operator. Haldane came hurrying to where Faustaff and Peppiatt were climbing down. He was fiddling with his helmet. Then his radio blasted on all the frequencies they were using.

'Alert! Alert! All guards to Area 50. D-squad about to attack adjustor.'

Also in Arrow Books by Michael Moorcock:

Elric of Melniboné

Michael Moorcock

THE RITUALS OF INFINITY

ARROW BOOKS

ARROW BOOKS LTD
3 Fitzroy Square, London W1

An imprint of the Hutchinson Publishing Group

London Melbourne Sydney Auckland
Wellington Johannesburg Cape Town
and agencies throughout the world

First serialised in *New Worlds* 1965–6
First published in book form by Arrow Books Ltd 1971
This edition 1975

Made and printed in Great Britain
by The Anchor Press Ltd
Tiptree, Essex

ISBN 0 09 910340 1

For Jimmy Ballard

When all the world dissolves,
And every creature shall be purified,
All place shall be hell that is not heaven.

Christopher Marlowe, *Doctor Faustus*

Prologue

There they lay, outside of space and time, each hanging in its separate limbo, each a planet called Earth. Fifteen globes, fifteen lumps of matter sharing a name. Once they might have looked the same, too, but now they were very different. One was comprised almost solely of desert and ocean with a few forests of gigantic, distorted trees growing in the northern hemisphere; another seemed to be in perpetual twilight, a planet of dark obsidian; yet another was a honeycomb of multicoloured crystal and another had a single continent that was a ring of land around a vast lagoon. The wrecks of Time, abandoned and dying, each with a decreasing number of human inhabitants for the most part unaware of the doom overhanging their worlds. These worlds existed in a kind of subspacial *well* created in furtherance of a series of drastic experiments . . .

1

The Great American Desert

In Professor Faustaff's code-book this world was designated as Earth 3. The professor steered his flame-red Buick convertible along the silted highway that crossed the diamond-dry desert, holding the wheel carefully, like the captain of a schooner negotiating a treacherous series of sandbanks.

The desert stretched on all sides, vast and lonely, harsh and desolate beneath the intense glare of the sun swelling at its zenith in the metallic blue sky. On this alternate Earth there was little but desert and ocean, the one a flat continuation of the other.

The professor hummed a song to himself as he drove, his bulk sprawling across both front seats. Sunlight glinted off the beads of sweat on his shiny red face, caught the lenses of his polaroid glasses and brightened those parts of the Buick not yet dulled by the desert dust. The engine roared like a beast and Professor Faustaff chanted mindlessly to its rhythm.

He was dressed in a Hawaiian shirt and gold beach-shorts, a pair of battered sneakers on his feet and a baseball cap tilted on his head. He weighed at least twenty stone and was a good six and a half feet tall. A big man. Though he drove with care his body was completely relaxed and his mind was at rest. He was at home in this environment as he was in more than a dozen others. The ecology of this Earth could not, of course, support human life. It did not. Professor Faustaff and his teams supported human life here and on all but two of the other alternates. It was a big responsibility. The professor carried it with a certain equanimity.

The capital of Greater America, Los Angeles, was two hours behind him and he was heading for San Francisco where he had his headquarters on this alternate Earth. He would be there the next day and planned to stop at a motel he knew en route, spend the night there, and continue in the morning.

Peering ahead of him Faustaff suddenly saw what appeared to be a human figure standing by the side of the highway. As he drove closer he saw that it was a girl dressed only in a swimsuit, waving at him as he approached. He slowed down. The girl was a pretty readhead, her hair long and straight, her nose fairly sharp and freckled. Her mouth was large and pleasant.

Faustaff stopped the car beside the girl.

'What's the trouble?'

'Truck driver was giving me a lift to 'Frisco. He dumped me when I wouldn't go and play amongst the cactus with him.' Her voice was soft and a trifle ironic.

'Didn't he realise you could have died before someone else came along?'

'He might have liked that. He was very upset.'

'You'd better get in.' Most young women

attracted Faustaff and the redhead particularly appealed to him. As she squeezed into the passenger seat beside him he began to breathe a little more heavily than usual. Her face seemed to assume a more serious expression as he glanced at her but she said nothing.

'My name's Nancy Hunt,' she said. 'I'm from L.A. You?'

'Professor Faustaff, I live in 'Frisco.'

'A professor—you don't look like a professor—a business man more, I guess, but even then—a painter, maybe.'

'Well, I'm sorry to say I'm a physicist—a physicist of all work you could say.' He grinned at her and she grinned back, her eyes warming. Like most women she was already attracted by Faustaff's powerful appeal. Faustaff accepted this as normal and had never bothered to work out why he should be so successful in love. It might be his unquestioning enjoyment of love-making and general liking for women. A kindly nature and an uncomplicated appreciation for all the bodily pleasures, a character that demanded no sustenance from others, these were probably the bases for Faustaff's success with women. Whether eating, boozing, smoking, love-making, talking, inventing, helping people or giving pleasure in general, Faustaff did it with such spontaneity, such relaxation, that he could not fail to be attractive to most people.

'What are you going to 'Frisco for, Nancy?' he asked.

'Oh, I just felt like travelling. I was with this swimming party, I got sick of it, I walked out on to the street and saw this truck coming. I thumbed it and asked the driver where he was going. He said 'Frisco—so I decided to go to 'Frisco.'

Faustaff chuckled. 'Impulsive. I like that.'

'My boyfriend calls me moody, not impulsive,' she smiled.

'Your boyfriend?'

'Well, my ex-boyfriend as from this morning I suppose. He woke up, sat up in bed and said "Unless you marry me, Nancy, I'm going now." I didn't want to marry him and told him so. He went.' She laguhed. 'He was a nice guy.'

The highway wound on through the barren world and Faustaff and Nancy talked until naturally they moved closer together and Faustaff put his arm around the girl and hugged her and a little later kissed her.

By late afternoon they were both relaxed and content to enjoy one another's company silently.

The convertible sped on, thudding tyres and pumping pistons, vibrating chassis, stink and all, sand slashing against the windscreen and the big yellow sun in the hot blue above. The vast, gleaming desert stretched for hundreds of miles in all directions, its only landmarks the few filling stations and motels along the rare highways, the occasional mesa and clumps of cactus. Only the City of Angels, in the exact centre of the desert, lay inland. All other cities, like San Francisco, New Orleans, Saint Louis, Santa Fe, Jacksonville, Houston and Phoenix, lay on the coast. A visitor from another Earth would not have recognised the continental outline.

Professor Faustaff chanted wordlessly to himself

as he drove, avoiding the occasional crater in the highway, or the place where sand had banked up heavily.

His chant and his peace were interrupted by a buzzing from the dashboard. He glanced at the girl and made a decision with a slight shrug of his shoulders. He reached inside the glove compartment and flicked a hidden switch there. A voice, urgent and yet controlled, began to come from the radio.

' 'Frisco called Professor F. 'Frisco calling Professor F.'

'Professor F. receiving,' said Faustaff watching the road ahead and easing off a little on the accelerator. Nancy frowned.

'What's that?' she asked.

'Just a private radio—I keep in touch with my headquarters this way.'

'Crazy,' she said.

'Professor F. receiving you,' he said deliberately. 'Suggest you consider Condition C.' Faustaff warned his base that he had someone with him.

'Understood. Two things. A U.M. situation is anticipated imminent on E-15, Grid areas 33, 34, 41, 42, 49 and 50. Representatives on E-15 have asked for help. Would suggest you use I-effect to contact.'

'It's that bad?'

'From what they said, it's that bad.'

'Okay. Will do so as soon as possible. You said *two* things.'

'We found a tunnel—or traces of one. Not one of ours. A D-squader we think. He's somewhere in your area, anyway. Thought we'd warn you.'

Faustaff wondered suddenly if he'd been conned

and he looked at Nancy again.

'Thanks,' he said to the radio. 'I'm arriving in 'Frisco tomorrow. Keep me informed of any emergency.'

'Okay, professor. Cutting out.'

Faustaff put his hand into the glove compartment again and flicked the switch off.

'Phew!' grinned Nancy. 'If that was a sample of the kind of talk you physicists go in for I'm glad I only had to learn Esperanto at school.'

Faustaff knew that he should feel suspicious of her but couldn't believe that she was a threat.

His 'Frisco office did not use the radio unless it was important. They had told him that an Unstable Matter Situation was imminent on the fifteenth and last alternate Earth. An Unstable Matter Situation could mean the total break-up of a planet. Normally, representatives of his team there could cope with a U.M.S. If they had asked for help it meant things were very bad. Later Faustaff would have to leave the girl somewhere and use the machine that lay in the trunk of his car—a machine called an invoker, which could summon one of Faustaff's representatives through the subspacial levels so that Faustaff could talk with him directly and find out exactly what was happening on Earth Fifteen. The other piece of information concerned his enemies, the mysterious D-squad who were, Faustaff believed, actually responsible for creating the U.M. Situations wherever they arose. A member —or members—of the D-squad were already on this Earth and could be after him. That was why he knew he should suspect Nancy Hunt and be cautious.

14

Her appearance on the highway *was* mysterious, after all, although he was still inclined to believe her story.

She grinned at him again and reached into his shirt pocket to get cigarettes and his lighter, putting a cigarette between his lips and cupping the flame of the lighter so that he was forced to bend his large head towards it.

As evening came and the sun began to set the sky awash with colours, a motel-hoarding showed up. The sign read:

LA PLEJ BONAN MOTELON
Nagejo—Muziko—Amuzoj

A little later they could just make out the buildings of the motel and another sign.

'PLUVATA MORGAU'
Bonvolu esti kun ni

Faustaff read Esperanto fluently enough. It was the official language, though few people spoke it in everyday life. The signs offered him the best motel, swimming, music and amusements. It had humorously been called The Rain Tomorrow and invited him to join the host.

Several more hoardings later they turned off the road into the car park. There were only two other cars there under the shade of the awning. One was a black Ford Thunderbird, the other was a white English M.G. A pretty girl in a frilly ballerina skirt that was obviously part of her uniform, a peaked cap on her head, strode towards them as they got stiffly out of the car.

Faustaff winked at her, his body dwarfing her. He put his sunglasses in his pocket and wiped his forehead with a yellow handkerchief.

'Any cabins?' he asked.

'Sure,' smiled the girl, glancing quickly from Faustaff to Nancy. 'How many?'

'One double or two singles,' he said. 'It doesn't matter.'

'Not sure we've got a bed to take you, mister,' she said.

'I curl up small,' Faustaff grinned. 'Don't worry about it. I've got some valuables in my car—if I close the roof and lock it will they be safe enough?'

'The only thieves in these parts are the coyotes,' she said, 'though they'll be learning to drive soon when they find that cars are all that's left to steal.'

'Business bad?'

'Was it ever good?'

'There are quite a few motels between here and 'Frisco,' Nancy said, linking her arm in Faustaff's. 'How do they survive?'

'Government grants mainly,' she replied. 'There've got to be filling stations and motels through the Great American Outback, haven't there? Otherwise how would anyone get to Los Angeles?'

'Plane?' the redhead suggested.

'I guess so,' said the girl. 'But the highways and motels were here before the airlines, so I guess they just developed. Anyway some people actually *like* crossing the desert by car.'

Faustaff got back into the car and operated the

hood control. It hummed and extended itself, covering the automobile. Faustaff locked it and got out again. He locked the doors. He unlocked the trunk, flipped a switch on a piece of equipment, relocked it. He put his arm around the redhead and said: 'Right, let's get some food.'

The girl in the cap and the skirt led the way to the main building. Behind it were about twelve cabins.

There was one other customer in the restaurant. He sat near the window, looking out at the desert. A big full moon was rising.

Faustaff and the redhead sat down at the counter and looked at the menu. It offered steak or hamburger and a variety of standard trimmings. The girl who'd first greeted them came through a door at the back and said: 'What'll it be?'

'You do all the work around here?' asked Nancy.

'Mostly. My husband runs the gas pumps and does the heavy chores. There isn't much to do except maintain the place.'

'I guess so,' said Nancy. 'I'll have a jumbo steak, rare with fries and salad.'

'I'll have the same, but four portions,' said Faustaff. 'Then three of your Rainbow Sodas and six cups of coffee with cream.'

'We should have more customers like you,' the girl said without raising an eyebrow. She looked at Nancy. 'Want anything to follow, honey?'

The redhead grinned. 'I'll have vanilla icecream and coffee with cream.'

'Go and sit down. It'll be ten minutes.'

They crossed to a window table. For the first time

17

Faustaff saw the face of the other customer. He was pale, with his close-cropped black hair growing in a widow's peak, a neat, thin black beard and moustache, his features ascetic, his lips pursed as he stared at the moon. He turned suddenly and glanced at Faustaff, gave a slight inclination of the head and looked back at the moon. His eyes had been bright, black and sardonic.

A little while later the girl came with the order on a big tray. 'Your other steaks are in that dish,' she said as she set it on the table. 'And your trimmings are in those two smaller dishes. Okay?'

'Fine,' Faustaff nodded.

The girl put all the contents of the tray on to the table and then stood back. She hesitated and then looked at the other customer.

'Anything else you want—er—Herr Stevel . . . sir . . . ?'

'Steifflomeis,' he said smiling at her. Although his expression was perfectly amiable, there was still a touch of the sardonic gleam Faustaff had seen earlier. It seemed to faze the girl. She just grunted and hurried back to the counter.

Steifflomeis nodded again at Faustaff and Nancy.

'I am a visitor to your country I am afraid,' he said. 'I should have invented some sort of pseudonym that could be more easily pronounced.'

Faustaff had his mouth full of steak and couldn't respond at once, but Nancy said politely: 'Oh, and where are you from, Mr. . . . ?'

'Steifflomeis,' he laughed. 'Well, my present home is in Sweden.'

'Over here on business or holiday?' Faustaff

asked carefully. Steifflomeis was lying.

'A little of both. This desert is magnificent isn't it?'

'Hot, though,' giggled the redhead. 'I bet you're not used to this where you come from.'

'Sweden does have quite warm summers,' Steifflomeis replied.

Faustaff looked at Steifflomeis warily. There was very little caution in the professor's make-up, but the little there was now told him not to be forthcoming with Steifflomeis.

'Which way are you heading?' asked the girl. 'L.A. or 'Frisco?'

'Los Angeles. I have some business in the capital.'

Los Angeles—or more particularly Hollywood, where the presidential Bright House and the Temple of Government were situated—was the capital of the Greater American Confederacy.

Faustaff helped himself to his second and third steaks. 'You must be one of those people we were talking about earlier,' he said, 'who prefer to drive than go by plane.'

'I am not fond of flying,' Steifflomeis agreed. 'And that is no way to see a country, is it?'

'Certainly isn't,' agreed the redhead, 'if you like this sort of scenery.'

'I am very fond of it,' Steifflomeis smiled. He got up and bowed slightly to them both. 'Now, please excuse me. I will have an early night tonight, I think.'

'Goodnight,' said Faustaff with his mouth half-full. Once again Steifflomeis had that secret look in his black eyes. Once again he turned quickly. He left the restaurant with a nod to the girl who was still behind the counter, fixing Faustaff's sodas.

When he had gone the girl came over and stood by their table.

'What you make of him?' she asked Faustaff.

Faustaff laughed. The crockery shook. 'He's certainly got a talent for drawing attention to himself,' he said. 'I guess he's one of those people who go in for making themselves seem mysterious to others.'

'No kidding,' the girl agreed enthusiastically. 'If you mean what I think you mean, I'm with you. He certainly gives me the creeps.'

'Which way did he drive in from?' Faustaff asked.

'Didn't notice. He gave an L.A. hotel as his address. So maybe he came from L.A.'

Nancy shook her head. 'No—that's where he's going. He told us.'

Faustaff shrugged and laughed again. 'If I read him right this is what he wants—people talking about him, wondering about him. I've met guys like him before. Forget it.'

Later the girl showed them to their cabin. In it was a large double bed.

'It's bigger than our standard beds,' she said. 'Just made for you, you might say.'

'That's kind of you,' Faustaff smiled.

'Sleep well,' she said. 'Goodnight.'

'Goodnight.'

The redhead was eager to get to bed as soon as the girl had left. Faustaff hugged her, kissed her and then stood back for a moment, taking a small, green velvet skull cap from his shorts' pocket and fitting

20

it on his head before undressing.

'You're crazy, Fusty,' giggled the redhead, sitting on the bed and shaking with amusement. 'I'll never make you out.'

'Honey, you never will,' he said, as he stripped off his clothes and flipped out the light.

Three hours later he was awakened by a tight sensation round his head and a tiny, soundless vibration.

He sat upright, pushing back the covers, and getting as gently as possible out of bed so as not to disturb the girl.

The invoker was ready. He had better lug it out into the desert as soon as possible.

2

Three Men in T-shirts

Professor Faustaff hurried from the cabin, carrying his huge naked bulk with extraordinary grace and speed towards the car park and his Buick.

The invoker was ready. It was a fairly compact piece of machinery with handles for moving it. He heaved it from the Buick's trunk and began hauling it out of the car park, away from the motel and into the desert.

Ten minutes later he squatted beneath the moon, fiddling with the invoker's controls. He set dials and pressed buttons. A white light blinked and went out, a red light blinked, a green light blinked, then the machine seemed still again. Professor Faustaff stood back.

Half-seen traceries of light now seemed to spring from the invoker and weave geometric patterns against the darkness. At length a figure began to materialise amongst them, ghostly at first but steadily becoming more solid. Soon a man stood there.

He was dressed in a coverall and his head was bandaged. He was unshaven and gaunt. He fingered the disc, strapped wrist-watch fashion to his arm, and said nothing.

'George?'

'Hello, professor. Where are we?—I got the call. Can you make it fast?—we need everybody at the base.' Georges Forbes spoke tonelessly, unlike his normal self.

'You really are in trouble there. Give me the picture.'

'Our main base was attacked by a D-squad. They used their disruptors as well as more conventional weapons, helicopters flying in low. We missed them until they were close. We fought back, but the bastards did their usual hit and run attack and were in and out again in five minutes—leaving us with five men alive out of twenty-three, wrecked equipment and a damaged adjustor. While we were licking our wounds they must have gone on to create a U.M.S. We're trying to fight it with a malfunctioning adjustor—but it's a losing battle. Four others just won't be enough. We'll get caught in the U.M.S. ourselves if we're not careful—then you can write off E-15. We need a new adjustor and a full replacement team.'

'I'll do my best,' Faustaff promised. 'But we've no spare adjustors—you know how long one takes to build. We'll have to risk shipping one from somewhere else—E-1 is the safest, I guess.'

'Thanks, professor. We've given up hope—we don't think you can do anything for us. But if you can do anything . . .' Forbes rubbed his face. He seemed so exhausted that he didn't really know where he was or what he was saying. 'I'd better get back. Okay?'

'Okay,' said Faustaff.

Forbes tapped the disc on his wrist and began to dematerialise as the E-15 invoker tugged him back through the subspacial levels.

Faustaff knew he had to get to 'Frisco quickly. He would have to travel tonight. He began to haul the invoker back towards the motel.

When he was quite close to the car park he saw a figure in silhouette near his Buick.

The figure seemed to be trying to open the car door. Faustaff bellowed: 'What d'you think you're trying to do, buster?' He let go of the invoker and strode towards the figure.

As Faustaff approached the figure straightened and whirled round and it wasn't Steifflomeis as Faustaff had suspected but a woman, blonde, tanned, with the shapely synthetic curves of a dressmaker's dummy—the kind of curves an older woman bought for herself. This woman seemed young.

She gasped when she saw the fat giant bearing down on her, dressed only in a green velvet skull cap, and she moved away from the car.

'You haven't any clothes on,' she said. 'You could be arrested if I screamed.'

Faustaff laughed and paused. 'Who'd arrest me? Why were you trying to get into my car?'

'I guess I thought it was mine.'

Faustaff looked at the English M.G. and the Thunderbird. 'It's not dark enough to make that kind of mistake,' he said. The big yellow moon was high and full. 'Which is yours?'

'The Thunderbird,' she said.

'So the M.G.'s Steifflomeis. I still don't believe you could make a mistake like that—a red Buick for a black Thunderbird.'

'I haven't broken into your car. I guess I was just peeking inside. I was interested in that equipment you've got in there.' She pointed to a small portable computer in the back seat. 'You're a scientist aren't you—a professor or something?'

'Who told you?'

'The owner here.'

'Here. I see. What's your name, honey?'

'Maggy White.'

'Well, Miss White, keep your nose out of my car in future.' Faustaff was not normally so rude, but he was sure she was lying, as Steifflomeis had been lying, and his encounter with George Forbes had depressed him. Also he was puzzled by Maggy White's total sexlessness. It was unusual for him to find any woman unattractive—they were always attractive in some way—but he was unmoved by her. Subconsciously he also realised that she was unmoved by him. It made him uncomfortable without realising quite why.

He watched her flounce on high heels back towards the cabins. He saw her enter one, saw the door close. He went to get his invoker and hauled it into the trunk, locking it carefully.

Then he followed Maggy White towards the cabins. He would have to wake Nancy and get going. The sooner he contacted his team in 'Frisco the better.

Nancy yawned and scratched her scalp as she climbed into the car. Faustaff started the Buick up and drove out on to the highway, changed gear and stepped on the accelerator.

'What's the rush, Fusty?' She was still sleepy. He had had to waken her suddenly and also wake the motel owner to pay him.

'An emergency in my 'Frisco office,' he said. 'Nothing for you to worry about. Sorry I disturbed you. Try and get some sleep as we drive, huh?'

'What happened tonight? You bumped into a girl or something in the car park. What were you doing out there?'

'Got a buzz from the office. Who told you?'

'The owner. He told me while he was filling the tank for you.' She smiled. 'Apparently you hadn't any clothes on. He thought you were a nut.'

'He's probably right.'

'I get the idea that the girl and that Steifflomeis character are connected—have they anything to do with this emergency of yours?'

'They just might have.' Faustaff shivered. He had no clothes but the shirt and shorts he wore and the desert night was cold. 'Might just be salvagers, but . . .' He was musing aloud.

'Salvagers?'

'Oh, just bums—some kind of con-team. I don't know who they are. Wish I did.'

Nancy had fallen asleep by the time dawn came. The rising sun turned the desert into an expanse of red sand and heavy black shadows. Tall cactus, their branches extended like the arms of declamatory figures, paraded into the distance; petrified prophets belatedly announcing the doom that had overtaken them.

Faustaff breathed in the cool, dawn smells, feeling sad and isolated suddenly, retiring into himself in the hope that his unconscious might produce some clue to the identities of Herr Steifflomeis and Maggy White. He drove very fast, egged on by the knowledge that unless he reached 'Frisco quickly E-15 was finished.

Later Nancy woke up and stretched, blinking in the strong light. The desert shimmered in the heat haze, rolling on for ever in all directions. She accepted the bizarre nature of the continent without question. To her it had always been like this. Faustaff had known it as very different five years before— when a big U.M.S. had only just been checked. That was something he would probably never fully understand—tremendous physical changes took place on a planet, but the inhabitants never seemed to notice. Somehow the U.M. Situations were accompanied by a deep psychological change in the people—similar in some ways, perhaps, to the mass delusions involving flying saucer spottings years before on his own world. But this was total hallucination. The human psyche seemed even more adaptable than the human phsysique. Possibly it was the only way the people could survive and protect their sanity on the insane planets of subspace. Yet the mass delusion was not always complete, but those who remembered an earlier state of existence were judged insane, of course. Even on a mass level things took time to adapt. What the inhabitants of Greater America didn't realise now, for instance, was that theirs was the only inhabited land mass, apart from one island in the Philippines. They still talked about foreign countries, though they would forget little by little, but the countries were only in their imagination,

27

mysterious and romantic places where nobody actually went. Steifflomeis had given himself away immediately he said he was from Sweden, for Faustaff knew that on E-3 a gigantic forest grew in the areas once called Scandinavia, Northern Europe and Southern Russia. Nobody lived there—they had been wiped out in the big U.M.S. which had warped the American continent too. The trees of that area were all grotesquely huge, far bigger than North American redwoods, out of proportion to the land they grew on. And yet these were one of the best results of the partial correction of a U.M.S.

On all the fifteen alternate Earths with which Faustaff was familiar Unstable Matter Situations had manifested themselves and been countered. The result of this was that the worlds were now bizarre travesties of their originals and the further back down the subspacial corridor you went the more unearthly were the alternate Earths. Yet many of the inhabitants survived and that was the important thing. The whole reason for Faustaff's and his team's efforts was to save lives. It was a good reason as far as they were concerned, even though it seemed they were fighting a slow, losing battle against the D-squads.

He was convinced that Steifflomeis and Maggy White were representatives of a D-squad and that their presence heralded trouble for himself, if not the whole of his organisation. 'Frisco might have some new information for him when he got there. He hoped so. His usual equanimity was threatening to desert him.

'Frisco's towers were at last visible in the distance. The road widened here and cactus plants grew thicker in the desert. Behind Frisco was the blue and misty sea, but the only ships in her harbour were coast-going freighters.

The sedate pace of 'Frisco compared to the frenetic mood he had left behind in L.A. made Faustaff feel a little better as he drove through the peaceful old streets that had retained a character that was somehow redolent of an older America, an America that had only really existed in the nostalgic thoughts of the generation which had grown up before the first World War. The streets were crammed with signs lettered in Edwardian style, there was the delicious smell of a thousand delicatessens, the tolling of the trolley cars echoed amongst the grey and yellow buildings, the air was still and warm, people sauntered along the sidewalks or could be seen leaning against bars and counters within the cool interiors of little stores and saloons. Faustauff liked 'Frisco and preferred it to all other cities in Greater America, which was why he had chosen to set up his headquarters here rather than in the capital of L.A. Not that he minded an atmosphere of noise, bustle and neurosis—in fact he rather enjoyed it—but 'Frisco had a greater air of permanence than elsewhere on E-3 so that psychologically at any rate it seemed the best place for his H.Q.

He drove towards North Beach and soon drew up beside a Chinese restaurant with dark-painted windows with gold dragons on them. He turned to the redhead.

'Nancy, how would you like a big Chinese meal

and a chance to wash up?'

'Okay. But is this a brush off?' She could see he didn't intend to join her.

'Nope—but there's that urgent business I must attend to. If I don't come in later, go to this address.' He took a small notebook from his shirt pocket and scribbled the address of his private apartment. 'That's my private place. Make yourself at home.' He handed her a key. 'And tell them you're a friend of mine in the restaurant.'

She seemed too tired to question him any further and nodded, getting out of the car, still in her swim-suit, and walking into the restaurant.

Faustaff went up to the door next to the restaurant and rang the bell.

A man of about thirty, dark-haired, saturnine, wearing a T-shirt, white jeans and black sneakers, opened the door and nodded when he saw Faustaff. There was a large old-fashioned clock-face stencilled on to the front of his T-shirt. It looked like any other gimmick design.

Faustaff said: 'I need some help with the equipment in the trunk. Anyone else here?'

'Mahon and Harvey.'

'I guess we can get the stuff upstairs between us. Will you tell them?'

The man—whose name was Ken Peppiatt—disappeared and came back shortly with two other men of about the same age and build, though one of them was blond. They were dressed the same, with the clock design on their T-shirts.

Helped by Faustaff they manhandled the electro-invoker and the portable computer through the door and up a narrow stairway. Faustaff closed the door behind them and kept an eye on the young men until they had set the equipment down in a small room on the first floor. The boards were bare and the room had a musty smell. They went up more uncarpeted stairs to the next floor which was laid out like a living room, with old, comfortable furniture untidily crammed into it. There were magazines and empty glasses littered about.

The three men in T-shirts flopped into chairs and looked up at Faustaff as he went to a 1920-style cocktail cabinet and poured himself a large glass of bourbon. He spooned ice-cubes into the drink and sipped it as he turned to face them.

'You know the problem they have on E-15.'

The three men nodded. Mahon had been the man who had contacted Faustaff the day before.

'I gather you're already arranging for a team to relieve the survivors?'

Harvey said: 'They're on their way. But what they really need is an adjustor. We haven't a spare —it'll be dangerous to let one go from another alternate. If a D-squad attacks a world without an adjustor—you can say goodbye to that world.'

'E-1 hasn't had an attack yet,' Faustaff mused. 'We'd better send their adjustor.'

'Your decision,' said Mahon getting up. 'I'll go and contact E-1.' He left the room.

'I'll want reports on the situation whenever possible,' Faustaff told him as he closed the door. He turned to the two others. 'I think I've been in touch with the people who made that tunnel you found.'

'What are they—salvagers or D-squaders?' Harvey asked.

'Not sure. They don't seem like salvagers and D-squaders usually only turn up to attack. They don't hang about in motels.' Faustaff told about his encounter with the pair.

Peppiatt frowned. 'That's not a real name—Steifflomeis—I'd swear.' Peppiatt was one of their best linguists. He knew the root tongues of all the alternates, and many secondary languages as well. 'It doesn't click. Just possibly German, I suppose, but even then . . .'

'Let's forget about the name for the time being,' Faustaff said. 'We'd better put a couple of people on to watching them. Two Class H agents ought to be okay. We'd better have recordings, photographs of them, everything we can get for a file. All the usual information—normal whereabouts and so on. Can you fix that, Ken?

'We've got a lot of Class H agents on retainer. They'll think it's a security job—Class H still believe we're some kind of government outfit. You might as well use half-a-dozen—they're available.'

'As many as you think. Just keep tabs on the pair of them.' Faustaff mentioned that they were probably in L.A. or 'Frisco judging by what they had said. Their cars shouldn't be hard to trace—he'd taken the numbers as he left the car park that morning.

Faustaff finished his drink and picked up a clipboard of schedules lying on a table. He flipped through them.

'Cargoes seem to be moving smoothly enough,' he nodded. 'How's the fresh-water situation here?'

'We'll need some more. They're recycling already, of course, but until we get those big sea-water condensers set up we'll have to keep shipping it in from E-6.' E-6 was a world that now consisted of virtually nothing but fresh-water oceans.

'Good,' Faustaff began to relax. The E-15 problem was still nagging him, though there was little he could do at this stage. Only once before had he experienced a Total Break-up—on the now extinct E-16—the planet that had taken his father when a U.M.S. got completely out of hand. He didn't like to think of what had happened there happening anywhere else.

'There's a new recruit you might like to talk to yourself,' Harvey said. 'A geologist from this world. He's at main H.Q. now.'

Faustaff frowned. 'This will mean a trip to E-1. I guess I'd better see him. I need to go to E-1, anyway. They'll want an explanation about the adjustor for one thing. They'll be nervous, quite rightly.'

'They sure will, professor. I'll keep you in touch if anything breaks with this Steifflomeis and the girl.'

'Have you got a bed free? I'll get a couple of hours sleep first, I think. No point in working tired.'

'Sure. The second on the left upstairs.'

Faustaff grunted and went upstairs. Though he could last for days without sleep, it was mainly thanks to his instinct to conserve his energy whenever he had the chance.

He lay down on the battered bed and, after a pang or two of conscience about Nancy, went to sleep.

3

Changing Times

Faustaff slept for almost two hours exactly, got up, washed and shaved and left the house, which was primarily living quarters for a section of his E-3 team.

He walked down towards Chinatown and soon reached a big building that had once been a pleasure house, with a saloon and a dance floor downstairs and private rooms for one night rental upstairs. Outside, the building looked ramshackle and the old paint was dull and peeling. A sign in ornate playbill lettering could still be made out. It read, somewhat unoriginally, The Golden Gate. He opened a side door with his key and went in.

The place was still primarily as it had been when closed down by the cops for the final time. Everything that wasn't faded plush seemed tarnished gilt. The big dance hall, with bars at both ends, smelt a little musty, a little damp. Big mirrors still lined the walls behind the bars, but they were fly-specked.

In the middle of the floor a lot of electronic equipment had been set up. Housed in dull metal casings, its function was hard to guess. To an outsider many of the dials and indicators would have been meaningless.

A wide staircase led from the floor to a gallery above. A man, dressed in standard T-shirt, jeans and sneakers, was standing there now, his hands on the rail, leaning and looking at the professor below.

Faustaff nodded to the man and began to climb the stairs.

'Hi, Jas.'

'Hi, professor.' Jas Hollom grinned. 'What's new?'

'Too much. They said you had a new recruit.'

'That's right.' Jas jerked his thumb at a door behind him. 'He's in there. It was the usual thing—a guy getting curious about the paradoxes in the environment. His investigations led him to us. We roped him in.'

Faustaff's team made a point of drawing its recruits from people like the man Hollom had described. It was the best way and ensured a high standard of recruits as well as a fair amount of secrecy. The professor didn't court secrecy for its own sake but didn't approach governments and declare himself simply because his experience warned him that the more officials who knew about him and his organisation the more spanners there would be in his organisation's works.

Faustaff reached the gallery and moved towards the door Hollom had indicated, but before he entered he nodded towards the equipment below.

'How's the adjustor working. Tested it recently?'

'Adjustor and tunneller both in good shape. Will you be needing the tunneller today?'

'Probably.'

'I'll go down and check it. Mahon's in the communications room if you want him.'

35

'I saw him earlier. I'll talk to the recruit.'

Faustaff knocked on the door and entered.

The new recruit was a tall, well-built, sandy-haired young man of about twenty-five. He was sitting in a chair reading one of the magazines from the table in the centre. He got up.

'I'm Professor Faustaff.' He held out his hand and the sandy-haired man shook it a little warily.

'I'm Gerry Bowen. I'm a geologist—at the university here.'

'You're a geologist. You found a flaw in the plot of the Story of the Rocks, is that it?'

'There's that—but it was the ecology of Greater America—not the geology—that bothered me. I started enquiring, but everybody seems to be in a half-dream when it comes to talking about some subjects. A sort of . . .'

'Mass hallucination?'

'Yes—what's the explanation?'

'I don't know. You started checking, eh?'

'I did. I found this place—found it was turning out a near-endless stream of goods and supplies of all kinds. That explained what was supporting the country. Then I tried to talk to one of your men, find out more. He told me more. It's still hard to believe.'

'About the alternates, you mean?'

'About everything to do with them.'

'Well, I'll tell you about it—but I've got to warn you that if we don't get loyalty from you after you've heard the story we do what we always do . . .'

'That's . . . ?'

'We've got a machine for brainwashing you painlessly—not only wiping your memory clean of what you've learned from us, but getting rid of that bug of curiosity that led you to us. Okay?'

'Okay. What happens now?'

'Well, I though I'd give you a good illustration that we're not kidding about the subspacial alternate worlds. I'm going to take you to another alternate— my home planet. We call it E-1. It's the youngest of the alternates.'

'The youngest? That seems a bit hard to figure.'

'Figure it out after you've heard more. There isn't much time. Are you willing to come along?'

'You bet I am!' Bowen was eager. He had an alert mind and Faustaff could tell that in spite of his enthusiasm his intellect was working all the information out, weighing it. That was healthy. It also meant, Faustaff thought, that it wouldn't take long for positive information to convince him.

When Faustaff and Gerry Bowen got down to the ground floor Jas Hollom was working at the largest machine there. A faint vibration could be felt on the floor and some indicators had been activated.

Faustaff stepped forward, checking the indicators. 'She's doing fine.' He looked at Bowen. 'Another couple of minutes and we'll be ready.'

Two minutes passed and a thin hum began to come from the machine. Then the air in front of the tunneller seemed full of agitated dust which swirled round and round in a spiral until delicate, shifting colours became visible and the part of the room immediately ahead of the tunneller became shadowy until it disappeared.

37

'Tunnel's ready,' Faustaff said to Bowen. 'Let's go.'

Bowen followed Faustaff towards the tunnel that the machine had created through subspace.

'How does it *work*?' Bowen asked incredulously.

'Tell you later.'

'Just a minute,' Hollom said, making an adjustment to the machine. 'There—I was sending you to E-12.' He laughed. 'Okay—*now*!'

Faustaff stepped into the tunnel and grabbed Bowen, pulling him in too. Faustaff propelled himself forward.

The 'walls' of the tunnel were grey and hazy, they seemed thin and beyond them was a vacuum more absolute than that of space. Sensing this Bowen shuddered: Faustaff could feel him do it.

It took ninety seconds before, with an itching skin but no other ill-effects, Faustaff stepped out into a room of bare concrete—a store-room in a factory, or a warehouse. Bowen said: 'Phew! That was worse than a ghost train.'

But for one large piece of equipment that was missing, the equipment in this room was identical to that in the room they'd just left. It was all that occupied the dully-lit room. A steel door opened and a short, fat man in an ordinary lounge suit came in. He took off his glasses, a gesture that conveyed surprise and pleasure, and walked with a light, bouncing step towards Faustaff.

'Professor! I heard you were coming.'

'Hello, Doctor May. Nice to see you. This is Gerry Bowen from E-3. He may be coming to work with us.'

'Good, good. You'll want the lecture room. Um . . .' May paused and pursed his lips. 'We were a bit worried by E-15 requisitioning our adjustor, you know. We have some more being built, but . . .'

'It was on my orders. Sorry, doctor. E-1 has never had a raid, after all. It was the safest bet.'

'Still, a risk. This could be the time they pick. Sorry to gripe, professor. We realised the emergency was acute. It's odd knowing at the back of your mind that if a U.M.S. occurs we've nothing to fight it with.'

'Of course. Now—the lecture room.'

'I take it you won't want to be disturbed.'

'Only if something bad crops up. I'm expecting news from E-3 and E-15. D-squad trouble on both.'

'I heard.'

The corridor seemed to Bowen to be situated in a large office block. When they reached the elevator he guessed that that must be what it was—outwardly, anyway.

The building was, in fact, the central headquarters for Faustaff's organisation, a multi-storey building that stood on one of Haifa's main streets. It was registered as the offices of the Trans-Israel Export Company. If the authorities had ever wondered about it, they hadn't done anything to let Faustaff know. Faustaff's father was a respected figure in Haifa—and his mysterious disappearance something of a legend. Perhaps because of his father's good name, Faustaff wasn't bothered.

The lecture room was appropriately labelled LEC- TURE ROOM. Inside were several rows of seats facing a small cinema screen. A desk had been placed to one side of the screen and on it was mounted a control console of some kind.

'Take a seat, Mr Bowen,' said Dr May as Faustaff walked up to the desk and squeezed his bulk into a chair. May sat down beside Bowen and folded his arms.

'I'm going to be as brief as I can,' Faustaff said. 'And use a few slides and some movie-clips to illustrate what I'm going to say. I'll answer questions, too, of course, but Dr May will have to fill you in on any particular details you want to know. Okay?'

'Okay,' said Bowen.

Faustaff touched a stud on the console and the lights dimmed.

'Although it seems that we have been travelling through the subspacial levels for many years,' he began, 'we have actually only been in contact with them since 1971—that's twenty-eight years ago. The discovery of the alternate Earths was made by my father when he was working here, in Haifa, at the Haifa Institute of Technology.'

A picture came on to the screen—a picture of a tall, rather lugubrious man, almost totally unlike the other Faustaff, his son. He was skinny, with melancholy, overlarge eyes and big hands and feet. He looked like the gormless feed-man for a comedian.

'That's him. He was a nuclear physicist and a pretty good one. He was born in Europe, spent some time in a German concentration camp, went to America and helped on the Bomb. He left America soon after the Hiroshima explosion, travelled around a little, had a job directing an English Nu-

40

clear Research Establishment, then got this offer to come to Haifa where they were doing some very interesting work with high-energy neutrinos. This work particularly excited my father. His ambition —kept secret from everyone but my mother and me—was to discover a device which would counter a nuclear explosion—just stop the bomb going off. A fool's dream, really, and he had sense enough to realise it. But he never forgot that that was what he would like to work on if he had the chance. Haifa offered him that chance—or he thought it did. His own work with high energy neutrinos had given him the idea that a safety device, at very least, could be built that would have the effect of exerting a correcting influence on unstable elements by emitting a stream of high energy neutrinos that on contact with the agitated particles would form a uniting link, a kind of shell around the unstable atoms which would, as it were, "calm them down" and allow them to be dealt with easily and at leisure.

'Some scientists at Haifa Tech had got the same idea and he was offered the job of directing the research.

'He worked for a year and had soon developed a device which was similar to our adjustors in their crudest form. In the meantime my mother died. One day he and several others were testing the machine when they made a mistake in the regulation of the particles emitted by the device. In fiddling with the controls they accidentally created the first "tunnel". Naturally they didn't know what it was, but investigation soon brought them the information of the subspacial alternative Earths. Further frenzied research, which paralleled work on the adjustor, the tunneller and the invoker, produced the knowledge of twenty-four alternate Earths to our own! They existed in what my father and his team called "sub-space"—a series of "layers" that are "below" our own space, going deeper and deeper. Within a year of their discovery there were only twenty alternatives and they had actually witnessed the total extinction of one planet. Before the end of the second year there were only seventeen alternates and they knew, roughly, what was happening.

'Somehow the complete disruption of the planet's atomic structure was being effected. It would start with a small area and gradually spread until the whole planet would expand into gas and those gasses drift away through space leaving no trace of the planet. The small disrupted areas we now call Unstable Matter Locations and are able to deal with. What at first my father thought was some sort of natural phenomenon was later discovered to be the work of human beings—who have machines that create this disruption of matter.

'Although my father's scientific curiosity filled him, he soon became appalled by the fantastic loss of life that destruction of these alternate Earths involved. Whoever was destroying the planets was cold-bloodedly killing off billions of people a year.

'These planets, I'd better add, all had similarities to our own—and your own, Mr Bowen—with rough-ly similar standards of civilisation, roughly similar governmental institutions, roughly similar scientific accomplishments—though all, in some way or another, had come to a dead end—had stagnated. We

42

still don't know why this is.'

A picture came on to the screen. It was not a photograph but an artist's impression of a world the same size as Earth, with a moon the same as Earth's. The picture showed a planet that seemed of a universally greyish colour.

'This is E-15 now,' Faustaff said. 'This is what it looked like ten years ago.'

Gerry Bowen saw a predominantly green and blue world. He didn't recognise it. 'E-1 still looks like this,' Faustaff said.

Faustaff flashed the next picture. A world of green obsidian, shown in close-ups to be misty, twilit, ghastly, with ghoul-like inhabitants.

'And this is what E-14 looked like less than ten years ago,' came Faustaff's voice.

The picture Bowen saw next was exactly the same as the second picture he'd seen—a predominantly green and blue world with well-marked continental outlines.

'E-13, coming up now,' said Faustaff.

A world of blindingly bright crystal in hexagonal structures like a vast honeycomb. Deposits of earth and water had been collected in some of the indentations. Movie films showed the inhabitants living hand to mouth existences on the strange world.

'E-13 as it was.'

A picture identical to the two others Bowen had already seen.

The pattern was repeated—worlds of grotesque and fantastic jungles, deserts, seas, had all once been like E-1 was now. Only E-2 was similar to E-1.

'E-2 is a world that seemed to stop short, in our

43

terms, just around 1960 and the expansion of the space programmes. You wouldn't know about those, even, since E-3 stopped short, as I remember, just after 1950. This sudden halting of all kinds of progress still mystifies us. As I said, a peculiar change comes over people as well, on the whole. They behave as if they were living in a perpetual dream and a perpetual present. Old books and films that show a different state to the one they now know are ignored or treated as jokes. Time, in effect, ceases to exist in any aspect. It all goes together—only a few, like you, Mr Bowen break out. The people are normal in all other respects.'

'What's the explanation for the changes of these worlds?' Bowen asked.

'I'm coming to that. When my father and his team first discovered the alternate worlds of subspace they were being wiped out, as I mentioned, rapidly. They found a way of stopping this wholesale destruction by building the adjustors, refinements of the original machines they'd been working on which could control the U.M. Situations where they occurred.

'In order to be ready to control the U.M.S. where and when it manifested itself, my father and his team had to begin getting recruits and had soon built up a large organisation—almost as large as the one I now have. Well-equipped teams of men, both physically and mentally alert, had to be stationed on the other alternates—there were fifteen left by then, not fourteen as now.

'Slowly the organisation was built up, not without some help from officials in the Israeli government of the time, who also helped to keep the activities of my father and his team fairly secret. The adjustors were built and installed on all the worlds. By means of an adjustor's stabilising influence they could correct, to come extent, a U.M.S.—their degree of success depending on the stage the U.M.S. had reached before they could get their machine there and get it working. Things are much the same nowadays. Though we can "calm down" the disrupted matter and bring it back to something approximately its original form, we cannot make it duplicate its original at all perfectly. The deeper back you go through the subspacial levels, the less like the original the planet is and the more U.M. Situations there have been. Thus E-15 is a world of grey ash that settles on it from thousands of volcanoes that have broken through the surface, E-14 is nothing but glassy rock, and E-13 is primarily a crystalline structure these days. E-12 is all jungle and so on. Nearer to E-1 the worlds are more recognisable—particularly E-2, E-3 and E-4. E-4 had it lucky—it stopped progressing just before the first world war. But it mainly consists of the British Isles and Southern and Eastern Europe now—the rest is either waste-land or water.'

'So your father founded the organisation and you carried it on, is that it?' Bowen asked from the darkness.

'My father died in the Total Breakup of E-16,' Faustaff said. 'The U.M.S. got out of control—and he didn't get off in time.'

'You said the U.M.S. weren't natural—that somebody caused them. Who?'

'We don't know. We call them the D-squad—the

45

Demolition Squad. They make it their business to attack our stations as well as creating U.M. Situations. They've killed many people directly, not just indirectly.'

'I must say it's hard to believe that such a complicated organisation as yours can exist and do the work it does.'

'It has built up over the years. Nothing strange about that. We manage.'

'You talk all the time about alternate Earths—but what about the rest of the universe. I remember reading the theory of alternate universes some years ago.'

'We're pretty sure that the only alternates are of Earth and the moon in some cases. It's a pity space-flight is not yet sufficiently sophisticated, otherwise we could put the theory to the test. My father reached this conclusion in 1985 when the second manned spaceship reached Mars and "disappeared". It was assumed it had gone off course into a meteor storm on its return flight. Actually it turned up on Earth 5—its crew dead due to the stresses of passing through subspace in a most unorthodox way. This seemed to prove that some distance beyond Earth there are no subspacial alternates. Whether this is a natural phenomenon or an artifical one, I don't know. There's a lot we don't understand.'

'You think there is a force at work, apart from you?'

'I do. The D-squad speaks of that. But though we've done some extensive checking up, we haven't found a trace of where they come from—though it must be from somewhere on E-1. Why they should murder planets—and more specifically the inhabitants of those planets—the way they do, I cannot understand. It is inhuman.'

'And what is your real reason for doing all this, professor, risking so much?'

'To preserve human life,' said Faustaff.

'That is all.'

Faustaff smiled. 'That's all.'

'So it's your organisation against the D-squad, basically.'

'Yes.' Faustaff paused. 'There are also the people we call salvagers. They came from several different alternates—but primarily from E-1, E-2, E-3 and E-4. At different stages they have discovered our organisation and found out what it does. Either they have found us out of curiosity, as you did, or stumbled upon us by accident. Over the years they have formed themselves into bands who pass through the subspacial alternates looting what they can and selling it in worlds that need it—using E-1 as their main base, as we do. They are pirates, free-booters using stolen equipment that was originally ours. They are no threat. Some people are irritated by them, that's all.'

'There's no chance that they are connected with these D-squads.'

'None. For one thing it wouldn't be in their interest to have a planet destroyed.'

'I guess not.'

'Well, that's the basic set-up. Are you convinced?'

'Convinced and overwhelmed. There are a few details I'd like filled in.'

'Perhaps Dr May can help you?'

47.

'Yes.'

'You want to join us?'

'Yes.'

'Good. Dr May will tell you what you want to know, then put you in touch with someone here who'll show you the ropes. I'll leave you now, if you don't mind.'

Faustaff said goodbye to Bowen and May and 'eft the little lecture room.

4

The Salvagers

Faustaff drove his Buick towards the centre of San Francisco where he had his private apartment. The sun was setting and the city looked romantic and peaceful. There wasn't much traffic on the roads and he made good speed.

He parked the car and walked into the old apartment house that stood on a hill giving a good view of the bay.

The decrepit elevator took him up to the top and he was about to let himself in when he realised he'd given his key to Nancy. He rang the bell. He was still wearing the beach shirt and shorts and sneakers he had been wearing the day before when he left Los Angeles. He wanted a shower and a change before anything.

Nancy opened the door. 'So you made it,' she smiled. 'Is the emergency over?'

'The emergency—oh, yes. It's in hand. Forget about it.' He laughed and put his arms around her, lifting her up and kissing her.

'I'm hungry,' he said. 'Is my icebox well stocked?'

'Very well-stocked,' she grinned.

'Well, let's have something to eat and go to bed.'

He had now forgotten about wanting a shower.

'That seems a good idea,' she said.

Later that night the phone started ringing. Faustaff woke up instantly and picked it up. Nancy stirred and muttered but didn't wake.

'Faustaff.'

'Mahon. Message from E-15. Things are bad. They've had another visit from the D-squad. They want help.'

'They want me, maybe?'

'Well, yes, I think that's about the size of it.'

'Are you at H.Q.?'

'Yes.'

'I'll be over.'

Faustaff put the phone down and got up. Once again he was careful not to disturb Nancy who seemed a good sleeper. He put on a black T-shirt and a pair of dark pants and socks, then laced up his old sneakers.

Soon he was driving the Buick towards Chinatown and not much later was in The Golden Gate, where Mahon and Hollom were waiting for him.

Hollom was working on the tunneller, his face screwed up in impatience.

Faustaff went behind the bar and reached under it, putting a bottle of bourbon and some glasses on the counter.

'Want a drink?'

Hollom shook his head angrily.

Mahon looked up from where he was intently watching Hollom. 'He's having trouble, professor. Can't seem to drive the tunnel deep enough. Can't reach E-15.'

Faustaff nodded. 'That's sure proof that a big D-squad is working there. It happened that time on E-6, remember?' He poured himself a large drink and swallowed it down. He didn't interfere with Hollom who knew as much about tunnellers as anyone and would ask for help if he needed it. He leant on the bar, pouring himself another drink and singing one of his favourite old numbers, remembered from when he was a youngster. 'Then take me disappearing through the smoke rings of my mind, down the foggy ruins of time, far past the frozen leaves, the haunted, frightened trees, out to the windy beach, far from the twisted reach of crazy sorrow . . .' It was Dylan's *Mr Tambourine Man*. Faustaff preferred the old stuff, didn't care much for modern popular music which had become too pretentious for his taste.

Hollom said tight-faced: 'D'you mind, professor? I'm trying to concentrate.'

'Sorry,' said Faustaff shutting up at once. He sighed, trying to remember how long it had taken them to break through to E-6 the last time there had been a heavy block.

Hollom shouted wildly, suddenly: 'Quick—quick —quick—I won't hold it long.'

The air in front of the tunneller began to become agitated. Faustaff put down his drink and hurried forward.

Soon a tunnel had manifested itself. It shimmered more than usual and seemed very unstable. Faustaff knew that if it broke down he would be alone in the depths of sub-space, instantly killed. Though pos-

51

sessing very little fear of death Faustaff did have a strong love of life and didn't enjoy the prospect of having to give up living. In spite of this he stepped swiftly into the subspacial tunnel and was soon moving along past the grey shimmering walls. His journey was the longest he had ever made, taking over two minutes, then he was through.

Peppiatt greeted him. Peppiatt was one of several volunteers who had gone with the replacement team to E-15. Peppiatt looked haggard.

'Glad to see you, professor. Sorry we couldn't use the invoker—it's busted.'

'You are having trouble.'

The invoker was a kind of subspacial 'grab', working on similar principles to the sister machines, that could be used primarily to pull agents out of U.M.S. trouble-spots, or get them through the dimensions without needing a tunnel. A tunnel was safer since the invoker worked on the principle of forming a kind of shell around a man and propelling it through the layers in order to break them down. Sometimes they resisted and didn't break down. Then a man 'invoked' was lost for good.

Faustaff looked around. He was in a large, natural cave. It was dark and the floor was damp, neon lighting sputtering on the walls, filling the cave with lurid light that danced like firelight. Pieces of battered electronic equipment lay everywhere, much of it plainly useless. Two other men were by the far wall working at something that lay on a bench. Cables trailed across the floor. Several more men moved about. They carried laser rifles, their power-packs on their backs. The rifles had been stolen from the U.S.

government on E-1 and technicians in Haifa were trying to mass-produce them, but hadn't had much success as yet. Faustaff's men were not normally armed and Faustaff had given no order to fight back at the D-squad. Evidently someone had decided it was necessary. Faustaff didn't like it, but he decided not to question the order now that it had been made. The one thing the professor ever seemed adamant about was the fact that like doctors their business was to save, not take, life. It was the entire *raison d'être* of the organisation, after all.

Faustaff knew that his presence on E-15 wasn't likely to serve any particular practical purpose since the men working here were trained to cope with even the most desperate situation, but gathered that he was needed for the moral support the men might get from thinking about it. Faustaff was not a very introspective man on the whole. In all matters outside of his scientific life he acted more according to his instinct than his reason. 'Thinking causes trouble,' was a motto he had once expressed in a moment of feeling.

'Where's everyone else?' he asked Peppiatt.

'With the adjustor. Areas 33, 34, 41, 42, 49 and 50 were calmed down for a while, but the D-squad came back. Evidently those areas form the key-spot. We're still trying to get them under control. I'm just going back there, now.'

'I'll come along.'

Faustaff grinned encouragingly at the men he passed on his way to the exit.

Peppiatt shook his head wonderingly. 'Their spirit's better already. I don't know what you do, professor, but you certainly manage to make people feel good.'

Faustaff nodded absently. Peppiatt operated a control beside a big steel door. The door began to slide back into the wall, revealing a bleak expanse of grey ash, a livid sky from which ash fell like rain. There was a stink of sulphur in the air. Faustaff was familiar with the conditions on E-15, where because of the volcanic upheavals almost everywhere on the planet, the people were forced to live in caves such as the one they'd just left. Their lives were fairly comfortable, however, thanks to Faustaff's cargoes brought from more fortunate worlds.

A jeep, already covered by a coating of ash, stood by. Peppiatt got into it and Faustaff climbed into the back seat. Peppiatt started the engine and the jeep began to bounce away across the wasteland of ash. Apart from the sound of the jeep the world was silent. Ash fell and smoke rolled in the distance. Occasionally when the smoke cleared a little the outline of an erupting volcano could be seen.

Faustaff's throat was clogged by the ash carried on the sulphurous air. It was a grey vision of some abandoned hell and infinitely depressing.

Later a square building, half buried in the ash, came in sight.

'That's one of our relay stations, isn't it,' Faustaff pointed.

'Yes. It's the nearest our 'copters can get to the main base without having a lot of fuel difficulties. There should be a 'copter waiting.'

A few men stood about outside the relay station. They were dressed in protective suits, wearing oxygen masks and heavy, smoked goggles. Faustaff couldn't see a 'copter, just a small hovercraft, a useful vehicle for this type of terrain. But even as they drew up, an engine note could be heard in the air above and soon a helicopter began to come down nearby, its rotors thrumming as it settled in the dust.

Two men ran from the station as the 'copter landed. They were carrying flapping suits, similar to those that all the men here wore. They ran up to the jeep.

'We'll have to wear these, I'm afraid, professor,' Peppiatt said.

Faustaff shrugged. 'Well, if we must.' He took the suit offered him and began to pull it over his bulk. It was tight. He hated feeling constricted. He slipped mask and goggles over his face. At least breathing and seeing were easier.

Peppiatt led the way through the clogging, soft ash to the helicopter. They climbed in to the passenger seats. The pilot turned his head. 'They're coming out with fuel pellets now. Won't be long.'

'How are things up at the U.M.S.?' Faustaff asked.

'Pretty bad, I think. There are some salvagers here—we've seen them once—drifting around like buzzards.'

'There can't be as much for them to salvage here.'

'Only spare parts,' the pilot said.

'Of course,' said Faustaff.

Using stolen or salvaged equipment belonging to Faustaffs' organisation, the salvagers needed to loot spare parts whenever possible. In the confusion following a major D-squad attack this could be done quite easily. Though they resented the salvagers,

Faustaff's team had orders not to use violence against them. The salvagers were apparently prepared to use violence if necessary, thus the going was pretty easy for them.

'Do you know which gang is here?' Faustaff asked as the 'copter was fuelled.

'Two gangs working together, I think. Gordon Ogg's and Cardinal Orelli's.'

Faustaff nodded. He knew both. He had encountered them several times before. Cardinal Orelli was from E-4 and Gordon Ogg was from E-2. They were both men whose investigations had led them to discover Faustaff's organisation and had worked for it for a while before going 'rogue'. Most of their gangs were comprised of similar men. Faustaff had a surprisingly few number of deserters and most of those were now salvagers.

The helicopter began to lift into the ash-laden air.

Within half-an-hour Faustaff could see signs of the U.M.S. ahead.

The Unstable Matter Situation was confined in a rough radius of ten miles. Here there was no grey ash, but boiling colour and an ear-shattering, unearthly noise.

Faustaff found it hard to adjust his eyes and ears to the U.M.S. He was familiar with the sight and sound of disrupted, unstable matter, but he never got used to it.

Great spiralling gouts of stuff would twist hundreds of feet into the air and then fall back again. The sounds were almost indescribable, like the roar of a thousand tidal waves, the screech of vast sheets of metal being tortured and twisted, the rumble of gigantic landslides.

Around the perimeter of this terrifying example of nature's death-throes there buzzed land-craft and helicopters. A big adjustor could be seen, trained on the U.M.S., the men and machines completely dwarfed by the swirling fury of the unstable elements.

They were now forced to use the radios in their helmets to speak to one another, and even then words were difficult to make out through the crackles of interference.

The helicopter landed and Faustaff got out, hurrying towards the adjustor.

One of the men near the adjustor was standing watching the instruments, arms folded.

Faustaff tapped him on the shoulder.

'Yes,' came a distant voice through the crackle.

'Faustaff—what's the situation like?'

'More or less static, professor. I'm Haldane.'

'From E-2 isn't it?'

'That's right.'

'Where are the original E-15 team—or what's left of them?'

'Shipped back to E-1. Thought it best.'

'Good. I hear you had another D-squad attack.'

'That's right—yesterday. Unusual intensity for them. As you know, they usually attack and run, never risk the chance of getting themselves hurt—but not this time. I'm afraid we killed one of them—died instantly—sorry to have to do it.'

Faustaff controlled himself. He hated the idea of

dying, particularly of violent death. 'Anything I can do here?' he asked.

'Your advice might be needed. Nothing to do at present. We're hoping to calm Area 50 down. We might do it. Ever seen something like this?'

'Only once—on E-16.'

Haldane didn't comment, although the implication must have been clear. Another voice came in. It was an urgent voice.

' 'Copter 36 to base—U.M.S. spreading from Area 41. Shift adjustor round there—and hurry.'

'We need another dozen adjustors,' Haldane shouted as he waved a hovering 'copter down to pick up the adjustor with its magnetic grab.

'I know,' Faustaff shouted back. 'But we can't spare them.' He watched as the grab connected with the adjustor and began to lift it up and away towards Area 41. Adjustors were hard to build. It would be folly to take others from more subspacial Earths.

The dilemma was insoluble. Faustaff had to hope that the one adjustor would finally succeed in checking and reversing the U.M.S.

A distorted voice that he eventually recognised as Peppiatt's voice said: 'What do you think, professor?'

He shook his head. 'I don't know. Let's get back to that 'copter and go round the perimeter.'

They stumbled back towards the 'copter and climbed in. Peppiatt told the pilot what to do. The 'copter rose into the air and began to circle the U.M.S. Looking it over carefully Faustaff could see that it was still possible to get the U.M.S. under control. He could tell by the colours. While the whole spectrum was represented, as it was now, the elements were still in their natural state at least. When they began to transform the U.M.S. would take on a purple-blue colour. When that happened it would be impossible to do anything.

Faustaff said: 'You'd better start getting the native population assembled in one place as soon as possible. We'll have to anticipate evacuation.'

'We won't be able to evacuate everyone,' Peppiatt warned him.

'I know,' Faustaff said tiredly. 'We'll just have to do what we can. We'll have to work out the best place to ship them to, as well. Perhaps an uninhabited land area somewhere—where they won't come in contact with the natives of another world. This has never happened before—I'm not sure what a meeting between two different populations would produce and we don't want more trouble than we have.' A memory of Steifflomeis popped into his mind. 'The Scandinavian Forests on E-3 might be okay.' Already, tacitly, he was accepting that E-15 was finished. He was half-aware of this but his mind was struggling against the defeatist attitude beginning to fill him.

Suddenly the pilot broke in. 'Look!'

About six 'copters in close formation were coming through the ash-rain in the distance. 'They're not ours,' the pilot said, banking steeply. 'I'm going back to the base.'

'What are they?' Faustaff asked.

Peppiatt answered. 'Probably D-squaders. Might be salvagers.'

'D-squaders! Again!' The D-squads rarely attack-

59

ed more than once after they had started the initial U.M.S.

'I think they're out to destroy E-15,' Peppiatt said. 'We'll have to defend, you know, professor. Lots of lives at stake.'

Faustaff had never quite been able to make the logical step which excused the taking of life if it saved life. His mind was slightly confused as he nodded and said, with a tight feeling in his chest, 'Okay.'

The 'copter landed near the adjustor and the pilot got out and spoke to Haldane the chief operator. Haldane came hurrying to where Faustaff and Peppiatt were climbing down. He was fiddling with his helmet. Then his radio blasted on all the frequencies they were using.

'Alert! Alert! All guards to Area 50. D-squad about to attack adjustor.'

Within seconds helicopters began to move in towards Area 50 and land, disgorging armed men.

Faustaff felt infinitely depressed as he watched them take up their defensive positions around the adjustor.

Then the D-squad 'copters began to come in.

Faustaff saw black-clad figures, seemingly faceless with black masks completely covering their heads. They had weapons in their hands.

The barely-seen lance of concentrated light from a laser rifle suddenly struck down from one of the leading D-squad 'copters. A man on the ground fell silently.

The guards around the adjustor began to aim a criss-cross lattice of laser-rays at the coming 'copters. The 'copters dodged, but one of them exploded.

Like tiny, lethal searchlights the beams struck back and forth. The fact that the D-squads used E-1 equipment for all their attacks indicated to Faustaff that that was their origin. The only device they had which Faustaff and his men didn't have was the Matter Disrupter. Faustaff could make out the 'copter which carried it, flying well behind the others and rather lower.

More of Faustaff's men fell and Faustaff could barely stop himself from weeping. He felt a helpless anger, but it never once occurred to him to strike back at the men who had done the killing.

Another 'copter exploded, another went out of control and flew into U.M.S. Faustaff saw it become incredibly luminous and then its outline grew and grew, becoming fainter as it grew, until it vanished. Faustaff shuddered. He wasn't enjoying his visit to E-15.

Then he saw several of his guards fall in one place and realised that the attacking D-squad were concentrating their fire. He saw laser beams touch the adjustor, saw metal smoulder and burst into white flame. The helicopters rose and fled away, their mission accomplished.

Faustaff ran towards the adjustor. 'Where's Haldane?' he asked one of the guards.

The guard pointed at one of the corpses.

Faustaff cursed and began checking the adjustor's indicator dials. They were completely haywire. The adjustor was still powered and its central core hadn't been struck, but Faustaff could see immediately that it would take too long to repair. Why had the D-squads intensified their attacks so much, risking their lives—indeed, losing their lives—to do so? It wasn't like them. Normally they were strictly hit-and-run men. Faustaff pushed this question from his mind. There were more immediate problems to be solved.

He switched his helmet mike to all frequencies and yelled. 'Begin total population assembly immediate. Operate primary evacuation plan. The U.M.S. is going to start spreading any time—and when that happens we won't have much notice before the whole planet breaks up.'

The 'copter with the grab began to move down towards the adjustor but Faustaff waved it away. The adjustor was heavy and it would take time to get it back to base. The evacuation of all the men from the area was more important. He told as much to the pilot over his radio.

Against the background of the vast, undulating curtain of disrupted matter, the team worked desperately to get out of the area, Faustaff helping men into 'copters and giving instructions wherever they were needed. There weren't enough 'copters to get everyone out at once. The evacuation would have to be organised in two lifts.

As the last of the 'copters took off, a handful of men, including Faustaff and Peppiatt, were left behind.

Faustaff turned to look at the U.M.S. with despair, noting that the spectrum was slowly toning down. It was the danger signal.

He looked back and saw some land vehicles bumping across the grey wasteland towards them. They didn't look like his organisation's jeeps or trucks. As they drew closer he could make out figures sitting in them, dressed in a strange assortment of costumes.

Sitting high in the back of one jeep was a man dressed in red—a red cap on his head, a red smock covering most of his body. He had a small oxygen mask over his nose and mouth, but Faustaff recognised him by his clothes. It was Orelli, leader of one of the biggest teams of salvagers. He had a laser-rifle pack on his back, and the rifle across his knees.

Peppiatt's voice came through the crackle of static in his earpiece. 'Salvagers. Not wasting much time. They must be after the adjustor.'

The remaining guards raised their weapons, but Faustaff shouted: 'No firing. The adjustor's no use to us. If they want to risk their lives salvaging it, it's up to them.'

Now Faustaff could make out a figure in a jeep just behind Orelli's. An incredibly tall, incredibly thin figure, in a green, belted jacket covered in ash, black trousers and ash-smeared jackboots. He carried a machine-gun. He had a mask but it hung against his chest. His face was like a caricature of a Victorian aristocrat's, with thin, beak-like nose, straggling black moustache and no chin. This was Gordon Ogg who had once ranked high in Faustaff's organisation.

The jeeps came to a halt close by and Orelli waved blandly to the little group standing near the ruined adjustor.

'Rights of salvage are ours, I think professor. I gather that *is* Professor Faustaff in the bulky suit and helmet. I recognise the distinguished figure.' He had to shout this through the noise of the raging U.M.S.

Orelli leapt down from the jeep and approached the group. Ogg did likewise, approaching at a loping gait reminiscent of a giraffe. While Orelli was of average height and inclined to plumpness, Ogg was almost seven feet tall. He cradled his machine-gun in his left arm and stepped forward, extending his right hand towards Faustaff. Faustaff shook it because it was easier to do that than make a display of refusing.

Ogg smiled vaguely and wearily, brushing back dirty, ash-covered hair. Except in extreme cases he normally scorned any kind of protective gear. He was an Englishman in love with the early 19th century mystique of what an Englishman should do and be, a romantic who had originally opposed Faustaff purely out of boredom inspired by the well-organised routine of Faustaff's organisation. Faustaff still liked him, though he felt no liking for Orelli, whose natural deceit had been brought to full flower by his church training on E-4. Even his high intelligence could not counter the rare loathing that Faustaff felt for this man whose character was so preternaturally cruel and treacherous. Faustaff found it bewildering and disturbing.

Orelli's eyes gleamed. He cocked his head to one side, indicating the adjustor.

'We noted the D-squad flying back to its base and gathered you might have an old adjustor you didn't want, professor. Mind if we look at it?'

Faustaff said nothing and Orelli minced towards the adjustor, inspecting it carefully.

'The core's still intact, I note. Seems mainly a

question of ruined circuits. I think we could even repair it if we wanted to—though we haven't much use for an adjustor, of course.'

'You'd better take it,' Faustaff said grimly. 'If you hang around talking you'll be caught by the U.M.S.'

Ogg nodded slowly. 'The professor's right, Orelli. Let's get our men to work. Hurry up.'

The salvagers instructed their men to begin stripping the adjustor of the essential parts they wanted. While Faustaff, Peppiatt and the rest looked on wearily, the salvagers worked.

Ogg glanced at Faustaff and then glanced away again. He seemed embarrassed momentarily. Faustaff knew he didn't normally work with Orelli, that Ogg despised the ex-cardinal as much as Faustaff did. He assumed that the difficulty of getting a tunnel through to E-15 had caused the two men to join forces for this operation. Ogg would have to be very careful that he was not betrayed in some way by Orelli when the usefulness of the partnership was over.

Faustaff turned back to look at the U.M.S. Slowly but surely the spectrum was toning down towards the purple-blue that would indicate it was about to spread in full force.

5

The Break-up of E-15

When the 'copters had returned and taken Faustaff
and the rest back to base, leaving the salvagers
still picking the bones of the adjustor, Faustaff immediately took charge of the evacuation plans. It
was proving difficult, he was informed, to get many
of E-15's natives to the central base. Being in ignorance of Faustaff and his team, they were suspicious
and reluctant to move. Some were already at the
base, gathered from the nearby underground com-
munities. Looking dazed and unable to comprehend
where they were and what was happening, they even
seemed to be losing touch with their own individual
identities. Faustaff was interested to see this, since it
gave him additional data on their reactions which
might help him understand the queer psychic
changes that took place amongst the populations of
the inhabitants of subspace. His detached interest in
their state didn't stop him from approaching them
individually and trying to convince them that they
were better off at the centre. He realised he would
have to put several sympathetic members of his team
in with their group when they were re-located on
E-3's gigantic forest areas.

With some difficulty the group had succeeded in putting a tunnel through to E-3. The evacuees were already beginning to be shuttled through.

In dribs and drabs they came in and were escorted through the tunnel. Faustaff felt sorry for them as they moved, for the most part, like automatons. Many of them actually seemed to think they were experiencing a strange dream.

Eventually the last of the evacuees were through and the team began to gather up its equipment.

Peppiatt was in charge of the tunneller and he began to look worried as the subspacial 'opening' flickered.

'Can't hold it open much longer, professor,' he said. The last few guards stepped forward into the tunnel. 'We're the last,' he said with some relief, turning to Faustaff.

'After you,' said Faustaff.

Peppiatt left the tunneller's controls and stepped forward. Faustaff thought he heard him scream as the tennel collapsed. He rushed back to the tunneller and desperately tried to bring the tunnel back to normal. But a combination of the subspacial blocks and the steadily increasing disruption on E-15 made it impossible. Eventually he abandoned the tunneller and checked the invoker-disc on his wrist. There wasn't much hope of that working, either, under these conditions.

It looked as if he was trapped on the doomed world.

Faustaff, as usual, acted instinctively. He rushed from the cavern-chamber and out to where a 'copter still stood. He had had some training in piloting the 'copters. He hoped he could remember enough of it. He forced his huge frame into the seat and started the engine. Soon he had managed to get the 'copter into the air. On the horizon the peculiar purple-blue aurora indicated that there was little time left before the whole planet broke up.

He headed east, to where he had gathered the salvagers had their camp. He could only hope that they hadn't yet left and that their tunnel was still operating. There was a good chance that even if that were the case they would refuse to help him get off the planet.

He could soon see the shimmering, light plastic domes of a temporary camp that must be that of the salvages. He could see no signs of activity and at first thought that they had left.

He landed and went into the first tent he came to. There were no salvagers there, but there were black-clad corpses. This wasn't the salvagers' camp at all —it was the camp of the D-squad. Yet as far as he could tell the D-squaders were dead for no apparent reason. He wasted time checking one of the corpses. It was still warm. But how had it died?

He ran from the tent and climbed back into the 'copter.

Now he flew even more urgently, until he saw a small convoy of jeeps moving below him. With some relief he realised that they had not yet even reached their base. They seemed to be heading towards a smoking volcano about ten miles away. He guessed that the salvagers had no 'copters on this operation. They were risking a lot in using the comparatively slow-moving turbojeeps. Had they killed the D-squaders? he wondered. If so, it still didn't explain how.

Soon he saw their camp—a collection of small inflated domes which he recognised as being made of the new tougher-than-steel plastic that seemed as flimsy as paper. It was used by the more advanced nations on E-1, mainly for military purposes.

Faustaff landed the 'copter with a bump that half-threw him from his seat. An armed guard, dressed in a heavy great-coat and a helmet that looked as if it had been looted from some 19th century fire station, moved cautiously towards him.

'Hey—you're Professor Faustaff. What are you doing here? Where are Ogg and Orelli and the others?'

'On their way,' Faustaff told the man, who seemed amiable enough. He recognised him as Van Horn, who had once worked for the organisation as a cargo control clerk. 'How's it going, Van Horn?'

'Not so comfortable as when I worked for you, professor, but more variety—and more of the good things of life, you know. We do pretty well.'

'Good,' said Faustaff without irony.

'Situation bad here, is it, professor?'

'Very bad. Looks like there's going to be a break-up.'

'Break-up! Phew! That is bad. Hope we get off soon.'

'It'll have to be soon.'

'Yes . . . What are you doing here, professor? Come to warn us? That's pretty decent.' Van Horn

69

knew Faustaff and knew he was capable of doing this.

But Faustaff shook his head. 'I've already done that. No—I came to ask for help. My tunneller went wrong. I'm finished unless I can get through your tunnel.'

'Sure,' Van Horn said with a grin. Like most people he liked Faustaff, even though his gang and Faustaff's organisation were somewhat opposed. 'Why not? I guess everybody will be pleased to help. For old time's sake, eh?'

'All except Orelli.'

'Except him. He's a poison snake, professor. He's so mean. I'm glad my boss is Ogg. Ogg's a weird guy, but okay. Orelli's a poison snake, professor.'

'Yes,' Faustaff nodded absently, seeing the jeeps approaching through the smoke and falling ash. He could make out Orelli in the leading jeep.

Orelli was the first salvager to encounter Faustaff. He frowned for a second and then smiled blandly. 'Professor Faustaff again. How can we help you?'

The question was rhetorical, but Faustaff answered directly. 'By giving me a chance to use your tunnel.'

'Our tunnel?' Orelli laughed. 'But why? Your father invented tunnellers—and now you come to us, the despised salvagers.'

Faustaff bore Orelli's amused malice. He explained how his tunnel had broken down. Orelli's smile grew bigger and bigger as he listened. But he said nothing.

Orelli looked like a cat who'd been handed a

mouse to play with. 'I'll have to talk this over with my partner, you understand, professor. Can't make a hasty decision. It could affect our whole lives in one way or another.'

'I'm asking you for help, man, that's all!'

'Quite.'

Gordon Ogg came loping up, looking vaguely astonished to see Faustaff there.

'What are you doing here, professor?' he asked.

'The professor is in trouble,' Orelli answered for him. 'Serious trouble. He wants to use our tunnel to get off E-15.'

Ogg shrugged. 'Why not?'

Orelli pursed his lips. 'You are too casual, Gordon. Too casual. "Why not?" you say. This could be a trap of some kind. We must be careful.'

'Professor Faustaff would not lay *traps*,' Ogg said. 'You are over-suspicious, Orelli.'

'Better safe than sorry, Gordon.'

'Nonsense. There is no question of the professor not coming through with us—assuming that we *can* get through.'

Faustaff saw Orelli's expression change momentarily to one of open anger and cunning, then the smile returned.

'Very well, Gordon. If you wish to be so reckless.' He shrugged and turned away.

Ogg asked Faustaff what had happened and Faustaff told him. Ogg nodded sympathetically. Originally some sort of British soldier-diplomat on E-2, Ogg's manner was gentle and remote and he was still an essentially kindly man, but the romantic mind of a Byron lay behind the mild eyes and courteous manner. Ogg saw himself, even if others did not quite see him in the same way, as a freebooter, a wild adventurer, risking his life against the warped and haunted landscapes of the subspacial alternates. Ogg lived this dangerous life and no doubt enjoyed it, but his outward appearance was still that of a somewhat vague and benign British diplomat.

Ogg led Faustaff to the main tent where his men were already going through the tunnel with their loot.

'The tunnel's to E-11,' Ogg said. 'It seemed no good in trying to get through to E-2 or E-1 under current conditions.'

'Perhaps we should have realised that,' Faustaff murmured, thinking of Peppiatt, dead in subspace. E-11 wasn't a pleasant world, being comprised primarily of high mountains and barren valleys, but he could contact his base on E-11 and soon get back to E-1.

Orelli came into the tent, smiling his brotherly love to everyone. 'Are we ready?' he asked.

'Just about,' said Ogg. 'The men have to collapse the other tents and get the heavy stuff through.'

'I think it might be wise to leave the rest of the jeeps behind,' Orelli said. 'The professor's prediction appears to have been accurate.'

Ogg frowned. 'Accurate?'

'Outside.' Orelli waved a hand. 'Outside. Look outside.'

Faustaff and Ogg went to the entrance of the tent and looked. A great, troubled expanse of purple-blue radiance filled the horizon, growing rapidly. Its edges touched a blackness more absolute than the

blackness of outer space. The grey ash had ceased
to fall and the ground close by had lost its original
appearance. Instead it was beginning to seethe with
colour.

Wordlessly Ogg and Faustaff flung themselves
back towards the tunneller. Orelli was no longer in
the tent. Evidently he hadn't waited for them. The
tunnel was beginning to look unsteady, as if about
to close. Faustaff followed Ogg into it, feeling sick
as he remembered Peppiatt's death earlier. The grey
walls flickered and threatened to break. He moved
on, not walking or propelling himself by any normal
means, but drifting near-weightlessly until, with relief, he found himself standing on a rocky mountain
slope at night time, a big, full moon above him.

Silhouetted in the darkness, other figures stood
around on the mountain side. Faustaff recognised
the outlines of Ogg and Orelli.

Faustaff felt infinitely depressed. E-15 would soon
be nothing more than fast-dissipating gas.

Even the salvagers seemed moved by their experience. They stood around in silence with only their
breathing to be heard. In the valley below Faustaff
could now make out a few lights, probably those of
the salvagers' camps. He was not sure where his
camp was in relation to his own base on E-11.

Faustaff saw a couple of men begin to climb down
the slope, feeling their way carefully. Others followed and soon the whole party was beginning to pick
its way down towards the camp, Faustaff in the rear.

At length they got to the valley and paused. Faustaff could now see that there were two camps—one
at either side of the short valley.

Ogg put his hand on the professor's arm. 'Come with me, professor. We'll go to my camp. In the morning I'll take you to your base here.'

Orelli gave a mock salute. 'Bon voyage, professor.' He led his men towards his own camp. 'I will see you tomorrow on the matter of spoil-division, Gordon.'

'Very well,' Ogg said.

Ogg's camp on E-11 had the same impermanent air as the hastily abandoned one on E-15. Ogg took Faustaff to his personal quarters and had an extra bed brought in for him.

They were both exhausted and were soon asleep in spite of the thoughts that must have occupied both their minds.

6

Steifflomeis on a Mountain

Just after dawn Faustaff was awakened by the sounds of activity in Gordon Ogg's camp. Ogg was no longer in the tent and Faustaff heard his voice calling orders to his men. It sounded like another panic. Faustaff wondered what this one could be.

He went outside as soon as he could and saw Ogg supervising the packing up of tents. A tunneller stood in the open air, and the salvager technicians were working at it.

'You're going through to another world,' Faustaff said as he reached Ogg. 'What's happening?'

'We've had word of good pickings on E-3,' Ogg said, stroking his moustache and not looking directly at Faustaff. 'A small U.M.S. was corrected near Saint Louis—but parts of the city were affected and abandoned. We can just get there before the situation's properly under control.'

'Who told you this?'

Ogg said: 'One of our agents. We have quite good communications equipment, too, you know, professor.'

Faustaff rubbed his jaw. 'Any chance of coming through your tunnel with you?'

Ogg shook his head. 'I think we've done you enough favours now, professor. We're leaving Orelli's share of the loot behind us. You'll have to make some sort of deal with him. Be careful, though.'

Faustaff would be careful. He felt somewhat vulnerable, being left to the doubtful mercies of Orelli, yet he had no intention of pressing Ogg to let him through the tunnel to E-3. He watched numbly as the salvagers got their equipment and themselves through the subspacial tunnel and then witnessed the peculiar effect as the tunneller itself was drawn through the tunnel it had created. Within seconds of the tunneller's disappearance, Faustaff was alone amongst the refuse of Gordon Ogg's camp.

Ogg had left him behind knowing that he ran fifty per cent risk of being killed outright by the malicious Orelli. Perhaps in Ogg's mind this was a fair chance. Faustaff didn't stop to wonder about Ogg's psychology. Instead he began to walk away from the camp towards the mountain. He had decided to try to make his way to his own base rather than trust Orelli.

By midday Faustaff had sweated his way through two crooked canyons and half-way up a mountain. He slept for an hour before continuing. His intention was to reach the upper slopes of the mountain, which was not particularly hard to climb and there was no snow to impair his progress. Once there, he would be able to get a better idea of where he was and plan his route. He knew that his base lay somewhere to the north-east of where he was, but it could be half-way around the world. Barren, and all-but completely covered by bleak mountain ranges though it might be, this planet was still Earth, with the same approximate size as Earth. Unless his base was fairly close, he couldn't give himself very good odds on his surviving for much more than a week. He still consoled himself that he was better off here than with Orelli and that there was a slim chance of search parties being sent out for him, though probably he was already thought to have been killed. That was the worst part of it. Without being self-important, he was aware that with him dead there was a good chance of his organisation losing heart. Though he did little but co-ordinate his various teams and advise where he could, he was an important figure-head. He was more than that—he was the dynamic for the organisation. Without him it might easily forget its purpose and turn its attention away from the real reason for its existence, the preservation of human life.

Sweating and exhausted Faustaff at last reached a point less than thirty feet from the mountain peak where he could look out over what seemed to be an infinity of crags. There were none he recognised. He must be several hundred miles from his base.

He sat down on the comparatively gradual slope and tried to reason out his predicament. Before long, he fell asleep.

He awoke in the evening to the sound of a muted cough behind him. Turning, unbelievingly, towards this human sound, he saw with some astonishment the dapper figure of Steifflomeis sitting on a rock just above him.

'Good evening, Professor Faustaff,' Steifflomeis

smiled, his black eyes gleaming with ambiguous humour. 'I find this view a trifle boring, don't you?'

Faustaff's depression left him and he laughed at the ludicrousness of this encounter. Steifflomeis seemed bewildered for a second.

'Why do you laugh?'

Faustaff continued to laugh, shaking his large head slowly. 'Here we were,' he said, 'with no human habitation to speak of in hundreds of miles . . .'

'That's so, professor. But . . .'

'And you are going to try to pass this meeting off as coincidence. Where are you on your way to now, Herr Steifflomeis? Paris? Are you just waiting here while you change planes?'

Steifflomeis smiled again. 'I suppose not. In fact I had a great deal of difficulty locating you after E-15 was eliminated. I believe E-15 is your term for that particular Earth simulation.'

'It is. Simulation, eh? What does that mean?'

'Alternate, if you like.'

'You're something to do with the D-squads, aren't you?'

'There is some sort of link between myself and the Demolition squads—an apt term that. Coined by your father wasn't it?'

'I think so. Well, what *is* the link? What are the D-squads? Who do they work for?'

'I didn't take the trouble of visiting this planet just to answer your questions, professor. You know, you and your father have caused my principals a great deal of trouble. You would never believe how much.' Steifflomeis smiled. 'That is why I am so reluctant to carry out their orders concerning you.'

'Who are your "principals"—what orders?'

'They are very powerful people indeed, professor. Their orders were for me to kill you or otherwise make you powerless to continue interfering in their plans.'

'You seem to approve of the trouble I have caused them,' Faustaff said. 'You're opposed to them, then? Some sort of—of double-agent? You're on my side?'

'On the contrary, professor—your aims and theirs have many similarities. I am opposed to both of you. To them, there is some purpose in all this creation and destruction. To me, there is none. I feel that everything should die—slowly, sweetly rotting away . . .' Steifflomeis smiled, more wistfully this time. 'But I am a dutiful employee. I must carry out their orders in spite of my own aesthetic fancies . . .'

Faustaff laughed, once again struck by the comedy of Steifflomeis's affectation. 'You are in love with death, then?'

Steifflomeis seemed to take the question as a statement carrying some sort of censure.

'And you, professor, are in love with life. Life, what is more, that is imperfect, crude, half-formed. Give me the overwhelming simplicity of death to *that*!'

'Yours seems a somewhat adolescent rejection of the tangle of being alive,' Faustaff said, half to himself. 'You could try to relax a bit—take it more as it comes.'

Steifflomeis frowned, his assurance leaving him even more, while Faustaff, calm, for some reason,

and in fairly good spirits, pondered on what Steifflomeis had said.

'I think you are a fool, Professor Faustaff, a buffoon. I am not the adolescent, believe me. My life-
span makes yours seem like the life-span of a
mayfly. You are naïve, not I.'

'Do you get no enjoyment from being alive, then?'

'My only pleasure comes from experiencing the
decay of the universe. It *is* dying, professor. I have
lived long enough to *see* it dying.'

'If that is true, does it matter to you or me?' Faustaff asked bemusedly. 'Everything dies eventually—
but that shouldn't stop us enjoying life while it is
there to be enjoyed.'

'But it has no purpose!' shouted Steifflomeis,
standing up. 'No purpose! It is all meaningless.
Look at you, how you spend your time, fighting a
losing battle to preserve this little planet or that—
for how long? Why do you do it?'

'It seems worthwhile. Have you no sympathy,
then, for the people who are destroyed when a planet
breaks up? It's a shame that they shouldn't have the
chance to live as long as possible.'

'But to what use do they put their stupid lives?
They are dull, fuddled, materialistic, narrow—life
gives them no real pleasure. The majority do not
even appreciate the art that the best of them have
produced. They are dead already. Hasn't that occurred to you?'

Faustaff debated this. 'Their pleasures are perhaps
a little limited, I'd agree. But they do enjoy themselves, most of them. And living is enough in itself.

It is not just the pleasures of life that make it worth-while, you know.'

'You talk like one of them. Their amusements are vulgar, their thinking obtuse. They are not worth wasting time for. You are a brilliant man. Your mind is tuned to appreciating things they could never appreciate. Even their misery is mean and limited. Let the simulations die, professor—let the inhabitants die with them!'

Again Faustaff shook his head in bemused amusement. 'I can't follow you, Herr Steifflomeis.'

'Do you expect their gratitude for this stupid dedication of yours?'

'Of course not. They don't realise what's going on, most of them. I am a little arrogant, I suppose, now that you mention it, to interfere in this way. But I am not a thinking man in most spheres, Herr Steifflomeis.' He laughed. 'You may be right—I am probably something of a buffoon.'

Steifflomeis seemed to pull himself together, as if Faustaff's admission had restored his assurance.

'Well, then,' he said lightly. 'Will you agree to let the planets die, as they must?'

'Oh, I'll continue to do what I can, I think. Assuming I don't starve out here, or fall off a mountain. This conversation is a little bit hypothetical when you consider my circumstances, isn't it?' he grinned.

It seemed rather incongruous to Faustaff that at that point Steifflomeis should reach into his jacket and take a gun out.

'You puzzle me, I admit,' said Steifflomeis. 'And I should like to watch you caper a little more. But since the moment is convenient and I have tiresome orders to carry out, I think I will kill you now.'

Faustaff sighed. 'It would probably be better than starving,' he admitted, wondering if there was any chance of making a dash at Steifflomeis.

7

Cardinal Orelli's Camp

In a manner that was at once studied and awkward, Steifflomeis pointed the gun at Faustaff's head while the professor tried to think of the best action to take. He could rush Steifflomeis or throw himself to one side, risking falling off the mountain ledge. It would be best to rush him.

He probably would not have succeeded if Steifflomeis hadn't looked up at the moment he ran forward, crouching to keep as much of his great bulk out of the line of fire as possible. Steifflomeis had been distracted by the sound of a helicopter engine above him.

Faustaff knocked Steifflomeis's gun to one side and it went off with a bang that echoed around the peaks. He hit Steifflomeis in the stomach and the bearded man went down, the gun falling out of his hand.

Faustaff picked up the gun and levelled it at Steifflomeis.

Steifflomeis frowned and gasped in pain. It was obvious that he expected Faustaff to kill him and a peculiar expression came into his eyes, a kind of introspective fear.

The helicopter was nearer. Faustaff heard it behind him and wondered who the pilot was. The noise of its engine became louder and louder until it deafened him. His clothes were ruffled by the breeze created by its rotors. He began to sidle round Steifflomeis, keeping him covered, so he could see the occupant of the helicopter.

There were two. One of them, wearing a smile of infinite cruelty, was the red-robed Cardinal Orelli, his laser rifle pointing casually at Faustaff's stomach. The other was a nondescript pilot in brown overalls and helmet.

Orelli shouted something through the roar of the motor, but Faustaff couldn't hear what he was saying. Steifflomeis got up from the ground and looked curiously at Orelli. Momentarily Faustaff felt more closely allied to Steifflomeis than to Orelli. Then he realised that both were his enemies and that Steifflomeis was much more likely to side with Orelli. Orelli must have come looking specifically for him, Faustaff decided, watching the pilot skilfully bring the helicopter down on the slope a little below him. Orelli's rifle was still pointing at him.

The engine noise died and Orelli climbed from the cockpit to the ground, walking up towards them, the fixed, cruel smile still on his lips.

'We missed you, professor,' he said. 'We were expecting you at our camp much earlier. You lost your way, eh?'

Faustaff could see that Orelli had guessed the truth; that he had deliberately chosen to enter the mountains rather than join the malicious ex-clergyman.

'I haven't had the pleasure,' said Orelli, turning a warier smile on Steifflomeis.

'Steifflomeis,' said Steifflomeis looking quizzical. 'And you are ... ?'

'Cardinal Orelli. Professor Faustaff calls me a "salvager". Where are you from, Mr Steifflomeis?'

Steifflomeis pursed his lips. 'I am something of a wanderer,' he said. 'Here today, gone tomorrow, you know.'

'I see. Well, we can chat at my camp. It is more comfortable there.'

Faustaff realised that there was little point to arguing. Orelli kept him and Steifflomeis covered as they walked down to the helicopter and climbed in, squeezing into the scarcely adequate back seats. With the gun cradled in his arm so that the snout pointed in their general direction over his shoulder, Orelli settled himself in the seat next to the pilot and closed the door.

The helicopter took the air again, banked and began to fly back in the direction from which it had come. Faustaff, grateful for his reprieve, though expecting a worse fate, perhaps, from Orelli, who hated him, looked down at the grim mountains that stretched, range upon range, in all directions.

Quite soon he recognised the valley, and Orelli's camp came into sight, the collection of grey dome-tents hard to make out against the scrub of the valley floor.

The helicopter descended a short distance from the camp and landed with a bump. Orelli climbed out and signalled for Steifflomeis and Faustaff to go ahead of him. They got down on to the ground and began to walk towards the camp, Orelli humming faintly what sounded like a Gregorian chant. He seemed in good spirits.

At Orelli's signal they bent their heads and entered his tent. It was made of material that permitted them to see outside without being visible themselves. There was a machine in the centre of the tent and Faustaff recognised it. He had also seen, once before, the two bodies that lay beside it.

'You recognise them?' Orelli asked casually, going to a large metal chest in one corner of the tent and producing a bottle and glasses. 'A drink? Wine only, I'm afraid.'

'Thank you,' said Faustaff, but Steifflomeis shook his head.

Orelli handed Faustaff a glass filled to the brim with red wine. 'St Emilion, 1953—from Earth Two,' he said. 'I think you'll find it pleasant.'

Faustaff tasted it and nodded.

'Do you recognise them?' Orelli repeated.

'The bodies—they're D-squaders, aren't they?' Faustaff said. 'I saw some like them on E-15. And the machine looks like a disrupter. I suppose you have plans to use it in some way, Orelli.'

'None as yet, but doubtless I shall have. The D-squaders are not dead, you know. They have been at a constant temperature ever since we found them. We must have passed through that camp of theirs on E-15 shortly before you. The body temperature is low, but not that low. Yet they aren't breathing. Suspended animation?'

'That's nonsense,' said Faustaff, finishing his drink. 'All the experiments tried in that direction have proved disastrous. Remember the experiments at Malmo in '91 on E-1? Remember the scandal?'

'I would not remember, of course,' Orelli pointed out, 'since I am not a native of E-1. But I read about it. However, this seems to be suspended animation. They live, and yet they are dead. All our attempts to wake them have been useless. I was hoping that you, professor, might help.'

'How can I help?'

'Perhaps you will know when you have inspected the pair.'

As they talked, Steifflomeis had bent down and was examining one of the prone D-squaders. The man was of medium height and seemed, through his black overalls, to be a good physical specimen. The thing that was remarkable was that the two prone figures strongly resembled one another, both in features and in size. They had close-cropped, light brown hair, square faces and pale skins that were unblemished but had an unhealthy texture, particularly about the upper face.

Steifflomeis pushed back the man's eyelid and Faustaff had an unpleasant shock as a glazed blue eye appeared to stare straight at him. It seemed for a second that the man was actually awake, but unable to move. Steifflomeis let the eyelid close again.

He stood up, folding his arms across his chest. 'Remarkable,' he said. 'What do you intend to do with them, Cardinal Orelli?'

'I am undecided. My interest is at present scientific—I wish to learn more about them. They are the first D-squaders we have ever managed to capture, eh, professor?'

Faustaff nodded. He felt strongly that the D-squaders should have fallen into any hands other than Orelli's. He did not dare consider the uses which Orelli's twisted mind could think of for the distrupter alone. With it he would be able to blackmail whole worlds. Faustaff resolved to destroy the disrupter as soon as he received a reasonable opportunity.

Orelli took his empty glass from his hand and returned to the metal chest, pouring fresh drinks. Faustaff accepted the second glass of wine automatically, although he had not eaten for a long time. Normally he could hold a lot of liquor, but already the wine had gone slightly to his head.

'I think we should return to my headquarters on E-4,' Orelli said. 'There are better facilities for the necessary research. I hope you will accept my invitation, professor, and help me in this matter.'

'I assume you will kill me if I refuse,' Faustaff replied tiredly.

'I would certainly not take it kindly,' smiled Orelli, sharklike.

Faustaff said nothing to this. He decided that it was in his interest to return to E-4 with Orelli since once there he would stand a much better chance of contacting his organisation once he had escaped.

'And what brought you to this barren world, Mr. Steifflomeis?' Orelli asked, with apparent heartiness.

'I had word that Professor Faustaff was here. I wanted to talk to him.'

'To talk? It appeared to me that you and the professor were engaged in some sort of scuffle as I came on the scene. You are friends? I should have thought not.'

'The argument was temporarily settled by your appearance, cardinal,' said Steifflomeis, his eyes matching Orelli's for cynical guile. 'We were discussing certain philosophical matters.'

'Philosophy? Of what kind? I myself have an interest in metaphysics. Not surprising, I suppose, considering my old calling.'

'Oh, we talked of the relative merits of living or dying,' Steifflomeis said lightly.

'Interesting. I did not know you were philosophically inclined, Professor Faustaff,' Orelli murmured to the professor. Faustaff shrugged and moved closer to the prone D-squaders until his back was to Steifflomeis and Orelli.

He bent and touched the face of one of the D-squaders. It was faintly warm, like plastic at room-temperature. It didn't feel like a human skin at all.

He had become bored with Orelli's and Steifflomeis's silly duelling. They evidently enjoyed it sufficiently to carry on with it for some time until Orelli theatrically interrupted Steifflomeis in the middle of a statement and apologised that time was running short and he must make preparations for a tunnel to be made through subspace to his headquarters on E-4. As he left the tent a guard entered, covering the two men with his gun. Steifflomeis darted Faustaff a sardonic look but Faustaff didn't feel like taking Orelli's place in the game. Although the guard would not let him approach too closely to the disrupter he contented himself with studying it from where he was until Orelli returned to say that a tunnel was ready.

8

The D-squaders

Even more tired and very hungry, Faustaff stepped through the tunnel to find himself in what appeared to be the vault of a church, judging by the Gothic style of the stonework. The stone looked old but freshly cleaned. The air was cold and a trifle damp. Various stacks of the salvagers' field equipment lay around and the room was lighted by a malfunctioning neon tube. Orelli and Steifflomeis had already arrived and were murmuring to one another. They stopped as Faustaff came up.

The D-squaders and the disrupter arrived soon after Faustaff, the prone D-squaders carried by Orelli's men. Orelli went ahead of them, opening a door at the far end of the vault and leading the way up worn, stone stairs into the magnificent interior of a large church, alive with sunshine pouring through stained glass. The only obvious change in the interior was the absence of pews. This gave the whole church an impression of being even larger than it was. It was a place that Faustaff could see easily compared to the finest Gothic cathedrals of Britain or France, an inspiring tribute to the creativeness of mankind. The church furniture remained, with a central altar and pulpit, an organ, and small chapels to left and right, indicating that the church had probably been Catholic. The wine was still affecting Faustaff slightly and he let his eyes travel up the columns, carved with fourteenth-century saints, animals and plants, until he was looking directly up at the high, vaulted roof, crossed by a series of intricate stone cobwebs, just visible in the cool gloom.

When he looked down again he saw Steifflomeis staring at him, a light smile on his lips.

Drunk with the beauty of the church Faustaff waved his hand around at it. 'These are the works of those you would have destroyed, Steifflomeis,' he said, somewhat grandiosely.

Steifflomeis shrugged. 'I have seen finer work elsewhere. This is pitifully limited architecture by my standards, professor—clumsy. Wood, stone, steel or glass, it doesn't matter what materials you use, it is always clumsy.'

'This doesn't inspire you, then?' Faustaff asked rather incredulously.

Steifflomeis laughed. 'No. You are naïve, professor.'

Unable to describe the emotions which the church raised in him, Faustaff felt at a loss, wondering to what heights of feeling the architecture with which Steifflomeis was familiar would raise him if he ever had the chance to experience it.

'Where is this architecture of yours?' he asked.

'In no place that you are familiar with, professor.' Steifflomeis continued to be evasive and Faustaff once again wondered if he could have any connection with the D-squads.

Orelli had been supervising his men. Now he

approached them. 'What do you think of my head-quarters?'

'Very impressive,' said Faustaff for want of something better to say. 'Is there more?'

'A monastery is attached to the cathedral. Those who live there follow somewhat different disciplines to those followed by the earlier occupants. Shall we go there now? I have a laboratory being prepared.'

'I should like to eat before I do anything,' Faustaff said. 'I hope your cuisine is as excellent as your surroundings.'

'If anything it is better,' said Orelli. 'Of course we shall eat first.'

Later the three of them sat in a large room that had once been the abbott's private study. The alcoves were still lined with books, primarily religious works of various kinds; there were reproductions framed on the walls. Most of them showed various versions of *The Temptation of St Anthony*—Bosch, Brueghel, Grunëwald, Schöngauer, Huys, Ernst and Dali were represented, as well as some others whom Faustaff did not recognise.

The food was almost as good as Orelli had boasted and the wine was excellent, from the monastery's cellar. Faustaff pointed at the reproductions. 'Your taste, Orelli, or your predecessor's?'

'His and mine, professor. That is why I left them there. His interest was perhaps a little more obsessive than mine. He went mad in the end, I hear. Some thought it possession, others . . .' he smiled his cruel smile and raised his glass somewhat mockingly to the Bosch—'delirium tremens.'

'And what caused the monastery to become deserted—why isn't the cathedral used now?' Faustaff asked.

'Perhaps it will be obvious if I tell you our geographical location on E-4, professor. We are in the area once occupied by North Western Europe. More precisely we are near where the town of Le Havre once stood, although there is no sign of the town and none of the sea, either, for that matter. Do you remember the U.M.S. that you managed to control in this area, professor?'

Faustaff was puzzled. He had not yet seen outside the monastery walls and where, logically, windows should look beyond the cathedral or the monastery, they were heavily curtained. He had assumed he was in some rural town. Now he got up and went to the window, pulling back the heavy velvet curtain. It was dark, but the gleam of ice was unmistakable. Beneath the moon, and stretching to the horizon, was a vast plain of ice. Faustaff knew that it extended through Scandinavia, parts of Russia, Germany, Poland, Czechoslovakia and parts of Austria and Hungary, covering, in the other direction, half of Britain as far as Hull.

'But there is ice for hundreds of miles about,' he said, turning back to where Orelli sat, sipping his wine and smiling still. 'How on earth can this place have got here?'

'It was here already. It has been my headquarters since I discovered it three years ago. Somehow it escaped the U.M.S. and survived. The monks fled before the U.M.S. developed into anything really spectacular. I found it later.'

'But I've never heard of anything quite like this,' Faustaff said. 'A cathedral and a monastery in the middle of a waste of ice. How did it survive?'

Orelli raised his eyes to the ceiling and smirked. 'Divine influence, perhaps?'

'A freak, I suppose,' Faustaff said sitting down again. 'I've seen similar things—but nothing so spectacular.'

'It took my fancy,' Orelli said. 'It is remote, roomy and, since I installed some heating, quite comfortable. It suits me.'

Next morning, in Orelli's makeshift laboratory, Faustaff looked at the two now naked D-squaders lying on a bench in front of him. He had decided that either Orelli was playing with him, or else Orelli believed his knowledge to extend to biology. There was very little he could do except what he was doing now, having electroencephalographic tests made on the subjects. It was not expedient to disabuse Orelli altogether, for he was well aware that, if there was no likelihood of his coming up with something, Orelli would probably kill him.

The skins still had the quality of slightly warm plastic. There was no apparent breathing, the limbs were limp and the eyes glazed. When the assistants had placed the electrodes on the heads of the two subjects he went over to the electroencephalograph and studied the charts that began to rustle from the machine. They indicated only a single wave a constant wave, as if the brain were alive but totally dormant. The test only proved what was already obvious.

Faustaff took a hypodermic and injected a stimulant into the first D-squader. Into the second he injected a depressant.

The electroencephalographic charts were exactly the same as the previous ones.

Faustaff was forced to agree with Orelli's suggestion that the men were in a total state of suspended animation.

The assistants Orelli had assigned to him were expressionless men with as little apparent character as the subjects they were studying. He turned to one of them and asked him to set up the X-ray machine.

The machine was wheeled forward and took a series of X-ray plates of both men. The assistant handed the plates to Faustaff.

A couple of quick glances at the plates were sufficient to show that, though the men on the table seemed to be ordinary human beings, they were not. Their organs were simplified, as was their bone structure.

Faustaff put the plates beside the D-squaders and sat down. The implications of the discovery swam through his mind but he felt unable to concentrate on any one of them. These creatures could have come from outer space, they could be a race produced on one of the parallel earths.

Faustaff clung to this last thought. The D-squaders did not function according to any of the normal laws applied to animals. Perhaps they *were* artificial; robots of some kind. Yet the science needed to create such robots would be far more advanced than Earth One's.

Who had created them? Where did they come from? The extra data had only succeeded in making everything more confusing than it had been.

Faustaff lit a cigarette and made himself relax, wondering whether to mention any of this to Orelli. He would discover the truth for himself soon enough anyway.

He got up and asked for surgical instruments. With the aid of the X-ray plates he would be able to carry out some simple surgery on the D-squaders without endangering them. He cut through to the wrist of one of them. No blood flowed from the cut. He took a bone sample and a sample of the flesh and the skin. He tried to reseal the incision with the normal agents, but they refused to take. Finally he had to cover the incisions with ordinary tape.

He took his samples to a microscope, hoping he had enough basic biology to be able to recognise any differences they might have to normal skin, bone and flesh.

The microscope revealed some very essential differences which didn't require any specialised knowledge for him to recognise. The normal cell structure was apparently totally absent. The bone seemed composed of a metal alloy and the flesh of a dead, cellular material that resembled foam plastic, although the cells were much more numerous than on any plastic he was used to.

The only conclusion he could draw from this evidence was that the D-squaders were not living creatures in the true sense and that they were, in fact, robots—artificially created men.

The appearance of the materials that had gone

into their construction was not familiar to Faustaff. The alloy and the plastic again indicated a superior technology to his own.

He began to feel perturbed for it was certain that the creatures had not been manufactured on any Earth that he knew. Yet they were capable of travelling through subspace and had obviously been designed for the sole purpose of manipulating the disrupters. That indicated the only strong possibility —that the D-squaders were the creation of some race operating outside subspace and probably from a base in normal space, beyond the solar system. The attack, then, probably did not come from a human source, as Faustaff had always believed. This was the reason for his uneasiness. Would it be possible to think out the motives of an unhuman race? It was unlikely. And without an indication of why they were trying to destroy the worlds of subspace, it seemed impossible to invent ways of stopping them for any real length of time.

He came to a decision then. He must destroy the disrupter, at least. It lay in one corner of the laboratory, ready for investigation.

To destroy it would at least stop Orelli using it, or threatening to use it in some attempt at blackmail. That would get rid of one of the factors bothering him.

He walked towards it.

At that moment he felt a tingling sensation on his wrist and the room seemed to fade. He felt sick and his head began to ache. He found it impossible to draw air into his lungs. He recognised the sensations.

He was being invoked.

9

E-Zero

Doctor May looked relieved. He stood wiping his glasses in the bare concrete room which Faustaff recognised as being in Earth One's headquarters at Haifa.

Faustaff waited for his head to clear before advancing towards May.

'We never thought we'd get you back,' said May. 'We've been trying for the last day, ever since you disappeared in the break-up of E-15. I heard our adjustor was destroyed.'

'I'm sorry,' said Faustaff.

May shrugged and replaced his glasses. His pudgy face looked unusually haggard. 'That's nothing compared to what's going on. I've got some news for you.'

'And I for you.' Faustaff reflected that May's invocation had come at exactly the wrong time. But it was no use mentioning it. At least he was back at his own base and could perhaps conceive a plan that would permanently put Orelli out of action.

May walked towards the door. Technicians were disconnecting the big invoker which had been used to pull Faustaff through subspace once they had picked up the signal from the invocation disc on his wrist.

Faustaff followed May out into the corridor and May led the way to the lift. On the fourth floor of the building they came to May's office.

Several other men were waiting there. Faustaff recognised some of them as heads of Central Headquarters departments and others he knew as communications specialists.

'Have you something to tell us before we begin?' May said, picking up a phone after introductions and greetings. He ordered coffee and replaced the phone.

'It won't take me long to fill you in,' Faustaff said. He settled himself into a chair. He told them of Steifflomeis's attempt to kill him and how it was plain that Steifflomeis knew much more about the worlds of subspace than he had admitted, that he had referred to his 'powerful principals' and indicated that the Faustaff organisation couldn't stand a big attack—and neither could the worlds of subspace. He then went on to describe Orelli's 'specimens' and what he had discovered about them.

The reaction to this wasn't as startled as he had expected. May simply nodded, his lips set tightly.

'This fits in with our discovery, professor,' he said. 'We have just contacted a new alternate Earth. Or I should say part of one. It is at this moment being formed.'

'An alternate actually being created!' Faustaff was excited now. 'Can't we get there—see how it happens. It could tell us a lot . . .'

'We've tried to get through to E-Zero, as we've

99

called it, but every attempt seems to have been blocked. This Earth isn't being created naturally—there is an intelligence behind it.'

Faustaff took this easily. The logical assumption now could only be that some non-human force was at work not only, as was now obvious, destroying worlds, but creating them as well. Somewhere the D-squaders, Steifflomeis and Maggy White fitted in —and could probably tell them a lot. All the events of recent days showed that the situation was, from their point of view, worsening. And the odds that faced them were bigger than they had guessed.

Faustaff helped himself to a cup of coffee from the tray that had been brought in.

Doctor May seemed impatient. 'What can we do, professor? We are unprepared for the attack, we are certainly ill-equipped to deal with even another big D-squad offensive of the kind you have just experienced on E-15. It is obvious that up to now these forces have been playing with us.'

Faustaff nodded and sipped his coffee. 'Our first objective must be Orelli's headquarters,' he said. He felt sick as he made his next statement. 'It must be destroyed—and everything that is in it.'

'Destroyed?' May was well acquainted with Faustaff's obsessive views about the sanctity of life.

'There is nothing else we can do. I never thought —I hoped I would never find myself in a situation like this, but we shall just have to follow the line of killing a few for the sake of the many.' Even as Faustaff spoke he heard his own voice of a short time ago talking about the dangers of justifying the taking of life under any conditions.

Doctor May seemed almost satisfied. 'You say he's on E-4. The area would be covered by grid sections 38 and 62 roughly. Do you want to lead the expedition? We shall have to send 'copters and bombs, I suppose.'

Faustaff shook his head. 'No, I won't go with it. Give them a five-minute warning, though. Give them that, at least. That won't allow them time to set up a tunneller and escape with the disrupter. I told you about the place—it'll be easy to spot, a cathedral.'

After Doctor May had gone off to arrange the expedition Faustaff sat studying the information that had so far been gathered about Earth Zero. There was very little. Apparently the discovery had been almost accidental. When E-15 was breaking up and it was becoming increasingly difficult to get tunnels between the worlds the technicians on E-1 found data being recorded on their instruments that was unusual. A check had led to contact with E-0. They had sent out probes and had found a planet that was still unstable, at that stage only a sphere consisting of elements still in a state of mutation. Soon after this their probes had been blocked and they had been unable to get anything but faint indications of the existence of the new body. All they really knew was that it was there, but they did not know how it had come there or who was responsible for it. Faustaff wanted to know *why* above everything else.

It was perhaps an unscientific attitude, he reflected as he got up. He had never before had quite such a strong sense of being unable to control a situation he found himself in. There was so little he could do at this stage. Philosophically he decided to give up and go to his house in the outer suburbs of Haifa, get a full night's sleep—the first he would have had in some time—hoping to have some ideas in the morning.

He left the building and walked out into the midday sunshine of the busy modern city. He flagged down a taxi and gave his address. Wearily he listened to the taxi-driver talking about the 'crisis' which seemed to have developed in his absence. He couldn't quite follow the details and made no serious attempt to, but it appeared that the East and West were having one of their periodic wrangles, this time over some South East Asian country and Yugoslavia. Since Tito's death Yugoslavia had been considered fair game for both blocs and although the Yugoslavs had steadfastly resisted any attempts at colonialism on the part of both East and West their situation was getting weaker. A revolution—from what appeared to be an essentially small group of fundamentalist Communists—had given the U.S.S.R. and the U.S.A. an excuse for sending in peace-keeping forces. From what the taxi-driver was saying there had already been open fighting between the Russians and the Americans and the Russian and American ambassadors had just withdrawn from the respective countries. Faustaff, used to such periodic events, was not able to feel the same interest in the situation as the taxi-driver. In his opinion the man was unnecessarily excited. The thing would die down eventually. It always had. Faustaff had more important things on his mind.

The taxi drew up outside his house, a small bungalow with a garden full of orange blossom. He paid the driver and walked up the concrete path to the front door. He felt in his pockets for the key, but as usual he had lost it. He reached up to the ledge over the door and found the spare key, unlocked the door, replaced the key and went in. The house was cool and tidy. He rarely used most of the rooms. He walked into his bedroom which was in the same state as he'd left it several weeks before. Clothes lay everywhere, on the floor and the unmade bed. He went to the window and opened it. He picked a towel off the television set that faced the foot of his bed and went into the bathroom. He began to shower.

When he returned, naked, to his room, there was a girl sitting on the bed. Her perfect legs were crossed and her perfect hands lay folded in her lap. It was Maggy White, whom Faustaff had encountered at the same time as he had first met Steifflomeis in the desert motel on E-3.

'Hello, professor,' she said coolly. 'Do you never wear clothes, then?'

Faustaff remembered that the first time he'd met her he had been naked. He grinned and in doing so felt immediately his old relaxed self.

'As rarely as possible,' he smiled. 'Have you come to try to do me in, too?'

Her humourless smile disturbed him. He wondered if making love to her would produce any real emotion. Her effect on him was far deeper than Steifflomeis's. She didn't reply.

'Your friend Steifflomeis had a bash at it,' he said. 'Or have you been in touch with him since then?

'What makes you think Steifflomeis is my friend?'

103

'You certainly travel together.'

'That doesn't make us friends.'

'I suppose not.'

Faustaff paused and then said: 'What's the latest news concerning the simulations.' The last word was one Steifflomeis had used. He hoped that he might trick her into giving him more information if he sounded knowledgeable.

'Nothing fresh,' she said.

Once again Faustaff wondered how a woman so well-endowed on the surface could appear to be so totally sexless.

'Why are you here?' he asked, going to the wardrobe and getting fresh clothes out. He pulled on a pair of jeans, hauling the belt around his huge stomach. He was putting on weight, he thought, the belt could hardly be pulled to the first notch.

'A social visit,' she said.

'That's ridiculous. I see that a new Earth is taking shape. Why?'

'Who can explain the secrets of the universe better than yourself, professor, a scientist?'

'You.'

'I know nothing of science.'

Out of curiosity Faustaff sat on the bed beside her and stroked her knee. Once again she smiled coolly and her eyes became hooded. She lay back on the bed.

Faustaff lay beside her and stroked her stomach. He noticed that her breathing remained constant even when he stroked her breasts through the cloth of her buttoned-up grey suit. He rolled over and stood up.

'Could you be Mark Two?' he asked. 'I dissected a D-squader a while ago. They're robots, you know —or androids, I think the term is.'

Perhaps he spotted a flash of anger in her eyes. They certainly widened for a moment and then half-closed again.

'Is that what you are? An android?'

'You could find out if you made love to me.'

Faustaff smiled and shook his head. 'Sweetheart, you're just not my type.'

'I thought any young woman was your type, professor.'

'So did I till I met you.'

Her face remained expressionless.

'What are you here for?' he asked. 'You didn't come because you felt randy, that's certain.'

'I told you—a social visit.'

'Orders from your principals. To do what, I wonder.'

'To convince you of the silliness of continuing this game you're playing.' She shrugged. 'Steifflomeis was unable to convince you. I might be able to.'

'What line are you going to take?'

'A reasonable one. A logical one. Can't you see that you are interfering with something that you will never understand, that you are just a minor irritant to the people who have almost total power over the parallels . . .'

'The simulations? What do they simulate?'

'You are dull, professor. They simulate Earth, naturally.'

'Then which Earth is it that they simulate. This one?'

'You think yours is any different from the others? They are all simulations. Yours was, until recently, simply the last of many. Do you know how many simulations there have been?'

'I've known of sixteen.'

'More than a thousand.'

'So you've destroyed nine hundred and eighty-six altogether. I suppose there were people on all of them. You've murdered millions!' Faustaff could not stop himself from feeling shocked by this revelation.

'They owed their lives to us. They were ours to take.'

'I can't accept that.'

'Turn on the television. Get the news,' she said suddenly.

'What for?'

'Turn it on and see.'

He went to the set and switched it on. He selected the English-speaking channel for convenience. Some people were being interviewed. They looked grim and their voices were dull with fatalism.

As Faustaff listened he realised that war must have been declared between the East and West. The men were not talking about the possible outcome. They were discussing which areas might survive. The general effect was that they didn't expected anywhere to survive.

Faustaff turned to Maggy White who was smiling again. 'Is this it? The nuclear war? I didn't expect it—I thought it was impossible.'

'Earth One is doomed, professor. It's a fact. While you were worrying about the other simulations your own was nearing destruction. You can't blame anyone else for this, professor. Who caused the death of Earth One .. ?'

'It must be artificially done. Your people must have ...'

'Nonsense. It was built into your society.'

'Who built it in?'

'They did, I suppose, but unknowingly. It is not in their interest, I assure you, to have this happen to a planet. They are hoping for a utopia. They are desperately trying to create one.'

'Their methods seem crude.'

'Perhaps they are—by their standards, but certainly not by yours. You could never comprehend the complicated task they have set themselves.'

'Who are they?'

'People. In the long run your ideals and theirs are not so different. Their scheme is vaster, that is all. Human beings must die. It is thought to be unfortunate by many of them. They aren't unsympathetic ...'

'Not unsympathetic? They destroy worlds casually, they let this happen—this war—when from all you say they could stop it. I can't have much respect for a race that regards life so cheaply.'

'They are a desperate race. They are driven to desperate means.'

'Haven't they ever—reflected?'

'Of course, many thousands of your years ago, before the situation worsened. There were debates, arguments, factions created. A great deal of time was lost.'

'I see. And if they are so powerful and they want

me out of the way, why don't they destroy me as they destroy whole planets? Your statements appear to be inconsistent.'

'Not so. It is a very complicated matter to eliminate individuals. It must be done by agents, such as myself. Usually it has been found expedient to destroy the whole planet if too many irritating individuals interfered in their plans.'

'Are you going to fill me in—tell me everything about these people. If I'm going to die because of a nuclear war, it shouldn't matter.'

'I wouldn't run the risk. You have a large share of pure luck, professor. I would suffer if I told you more and you escaped.'

'How would they punish you?'

'I'm sorry. I've told you enough.' She spoke rapidly, for the first time.

'So I'm to die. Then why did you come here to dissuade me if you knew what was going to happen?'

'As I said, you may not die. You are lucky. Can't you simply accept that you are complicating a situation involving matters that are completely above your head? Can't you accept that there is a greater purpose to all this?'

'I can't accept death as a necessary evil, if that's what you mean—or premature death, anyway.'

'Your moralising is naïve—cheap.'

'That's what your friend Steifflomeis says. But is isn't to me. I'm a simple man, Miss White.'

She shrugged. 'You will never understand, will you?'

'I don't know what you mean.'

'That's what I mean.'

'Why didn't you kill me, anyway?' He turned away and began to put on a shirt. The television continued to drone on, the voices becoming hollower and hollower. 'You had the opportunity. I didn't know you were in the house.'

'Both Steifflomeis and myself have a fairly free hand in how we handle problems. I was curious about these worlds, particularly about you. I have never been made love to.' She got up and came towards him. 'I had heard that you were good at it.'

'Only when I enjoy it. It seems odd that these people of yours understand little of human psychology from what I've gathered.'

'Do you understand the psychology of a frog in any detail?'

'A frog's psychology is a considerably simpler thing than a person's.'

'Not to a creature with a much more complex psychology than a person's.'

'I'm tired of this, Miss White. I must get back to my headquarters. You can write me off as an irritant from now on. I don't expect my organisation to survive the coming war.'

'I expected you to escape to some other simulation. It would give you a respite anyway.'

He looked at her curiously. She had sounded almost animated, almost concerned for him.

In a softer tone he said: 'Are you suggesting that?'

'If you like.'

He frowned, looking into her eyes. For some reason he suddenly felt sympathy for her without knowing why.

109

'You'd better get going yourself,' he said tersely, turning and making for the door.

The streets outside were deserted. This was unusual for the time of day. A bus stopped nearby. He ran to catch it. It would take him close to his headquarters. He was the only person on the bus apart from the driver.

He felt lonely as they drove into Haifa.

10

Escape from E-1

Faustaff and Dr May watched as men and equipment were hurried through the tunnel which had
been made to E-3. The expression on May's face was
one of hopelessness. The bombs had already started
to drop and the last report they had seen had told
them that Britain had been totally destroyed, as had
half of Europe.

They had given themselves an hour to evacuate
everything and everyone they could. Doctor May
checked his watch and glanced at Faustaff.

'Time's up, professor.'

Faustaff nodded and followed May into the tunnel. It took a great deal to depress him, but to see the
organisation he and his father had built up crumbling, forced to abandon its main centre, made him
miserable and unable to think clearly.

The trip through the grey tunnel to the familiar
gilt and plush dance hall of The Golden Gate which
was their main transceiving station on E-3, was
easily made. When they arrived, the men just stood
around, murmuring to one another and glancing at
Faustaff; he knew that he was expected to cheer
them up. He forced himself out of his mood and
smiled.

'We all need a drink,' was the only thing he could think of to say as he walked towards the dusty bar. He leaned across it and reached under, finding bottles and glasses and setting them on the counter. The men moved forward and took the glasses he filled for them.

Faustaff hauled himself up so that he was sitting on the bar.

'We're in a pretty desperate situation,' he told them. 'The enemy—I've hardly any better idea of them than you have—have for some reason decided to launch an all-out attack on the subspacial worlds. It's plain now that all their previous attacks, using the D-squaders, have hardly been serious. We underestimated the opposition, if you like. Frankly my own opinion is that it won't be long before they succeed in breaking up all the subspacial alternates —that's what they want.'

'Then there's nothing we can do,' Doctor May said wearily.

'Only one thing occurs to me,' Faustaff said. 'We know that the enemy considers these worlds as something to be destroyed. But what about E-Zero? This has just been created—either by them or by someone else like them—and I gather they aren't normally willing to destroy a recently created world. Our only chance is in getting a big tunnel through to E-Zero and setting up our headquarters there. From then on we can evacuate people from these worlds to E-Zero.'

'But what if E-Zero can't support so many?' a man said.

'It will have to.' Faustaff drained his glass. 'As far

112

as I can see our only course of action is to concentrate everything on getting a tunnel through to E-Zero.'

Doctor May shook his head, staring at the floor. 'I don't see the point,' he said. 'We're beaten. We're going to die sooner or later with everyone else. Why don't we just give up now?'

Faustaff nodded sympathetically. 'I understand— but we've got our responsibilities. We all took those on when we joined the organisation.'

'That was before we knew the extent of what we'd let ourselves in for,' May said sharply.

'Possibly. But what's the point of being fatalistic at this stage? If we're due to be wiped out, we might at least try the only chance we have.'

'And what then?' May looked up. He seemed angry now. 'A few more days before the enemy decides to destroy E-Zero? Count me out, professor.'

'Very well.' Faustaff glanced at the others. 'Who feels the same as Doctor May?'

More than half of the men there indicated that they shared May's views. At least half of the remainder seemed undecided.

'Very well,' he said again. 'It's probably best that we sorted this out now. Everyone who is ready to start work can remain here. The rest can leave. Some of you will be familiar with E-3, perhaps you can look after those who aren't.'

When May and the others had left, Faustaff spoke to his chief of Communications on E-3, John Mahon, telling him to call in all operatives from the other subspacial alternates and get them working on an attempt to break through to E-Zero.

Class H agents—those who worked for the organisation without realising what it was—were to be paid off. When Faustaff brought up the subject of Class H, Mahon snapped his fingers. 'That reminds me,' he said. 'You remember I put some Class H men on to checking up on Steifflomeis and Maggy White?'

It seemed a long time ago. Faustaff nodded. 'I suppose nothing came of it.'

'The only information we got indicates that they have a tunneller of their own—or at least some method of travelling through the subspacial levels. Two Class H agents followed them out to L.A. to a cottage they evidently use as their base on E-3. They never came out of that cottage, and a check showed that they weren't there. The agents reported finding a lot of electronic equipment they couldn't recognise.'

'It fits with what I found out,' Faustaff said. He told Mahon about his encounters with the two. 'If only we could get them to give us more information we might stand a better chance of getting a concrete solution to this mess.'

Mahon agreed. 'It might be worth going out to this cottage of theirs, if we could find the time. What do you think?'

Faustaff debated. 'I'm not sure. There's every likelihood that they'd have removed their equipment by now anyway.'

'Right,' said Mahon. 'I'll forget about it. We can't spare anyone now to go out and have a look for us.'

Faustaff picked up a tin box. It contained the information gathered about E-Zero. He told Mahon

114

that he was going to his apartment to go through it again and could be contacted there.

He drove his Buick through the sunny streets of Frisco, his enjoyment of the city's atmosphere now somewhat tainted by his mood of unaccustomed grimness.

It was only as he entered his apartment and saw how tidy the place was that he remembered Nancy Hunt. She wasn't there now. He wondered if she had given him up and left, although the indications were that she was only out temporarily

He went to his desk and settled down to work, the phone beside him. As he studied the data, he phoned ideas through to his team at The Golden Gate.

Nancy came in around midnight.

'Fusty! Where have you been? You look dreadful. What's been happening?'

'A lot. Can you make me some coffee, Nancy?'

'Sure.'

The redhead went straight into the kitchen and came out later with coffee and doughnuts. 'Want a sandwich, Fusty? There's Danish salami and liver sausage, rye bread and some potato salad.'

'Make me a few,' he said. 'I'd forgotten I was hungry.'

'There must be something important up, then,' she said, laying the tray down on a table near him and returning to the kitchen.

Faustaff thought there might be a way of creating a new kind of warp in subspace, something they'd thought of in the past but dismissed since their methods had then been adequate. He phoned

115

through to The Golden Gate and spoke to Mahon about it, telling him to find all the notes that had been made at the time. He realised that it was going to be several days before anything could be worked out properly and more time would be wasted in adapting the tunnelers, but his team was good, if depleted, and if anything could be done, they'd do it.

His brain was beginning to get fuzzy and he realised he would have to relax for a while before continuing. When Nancy came back with the sandwiches he went and sat next to her on the couch, kissed her and ate his way through the food. He sat back feeling better.

'What have you been doing, Nancy?'

'Hanging around, waiting for you. I went to see a movie today.'

'What was it about?'

'Cowboys. What have *you* been doing, Fusty? I was worried.'

'Travelling,' he said. 'Urgent business, you know.'

'You could have phoned.'

'Not from where I was.'

'Well, let's go to bed now and make up for all that time wasted.'

He felt even more miserable. 'I can't,' he said. 'I've got to go on with what I'm doing. I'm sorry, Nancy.'

'What's all this about, Fusty?' She stroked his arm sympathetically. 'You're really upset, aren't you? It's not just a business problem.'

'Yes, I'm upset. D'you want to hear the whole story?' He realised that he needed Nancy's comforting. There would be no harm now in telling her the whole story. Briefly he outlined the situation.

When he'd finished she looked incredulous. 'I believe you,' she said. 'But I can't—can't take it all in. So we're all going to die, is that it?'

'Unless I can do something about it. Even then, most of us will be destroyed.' The phone began to ring. He picked it up. It was Mahon. 'Hello, Mahon. What is it?'

'We're checking the new warp theory. It seems to be getting somewhere, but that wasn't why I called. Just thought I'd better tell you that E-14 and E-13 are in Total Break-up. You were right. The enemy's getting busy. What can we do?'

Faustaff sighed. 'Assign emergency teams to evacuate as many as possible from the deeper worlds. Evidently the enemy are working systematically. We'll just have to hope we can consolidate on here and E-2 and make a fight of it. Better order all the adjustors brought to E-2 and E-3. We'll spread them out. There might be a chance. We'll have to fight.'

'There was one other thing,' Mahon said. 'I think May organised an expedition to E-4 before you left E-1.'

'That's right. They were going to bomb Orelli's headquarters. Were they successful?'

'They couldn't find it. They came back.'

'But they must have found it—they couldn't have missed it.'

'The only thing they found was a crater in the ice. It could just be that the whole cathedral had vanished—been shifted. You said Steifflomeis was with

117

them, they had two D-squaders and a disrupter. It could easily mean that Steifflomeis is helping Orelli. He probably knows the potentialities of the disrupter. Or maybe something went wrong and the cathedral was destroyed in some way. The only thing that's certain is that they've vanished.'

'I don't think they've destroyed themselves,' Faustaff replied. 'I think we'll have to watch for them in the near future. The combination of Orelli and Steifflomeis is a bad one for us.'

'I won't forget. And I'll get the evacuation scheme moving. Any more details for us?'

Faustaff felt guilty. He'd spent too much time talking to Nancy.

'I'll let you know,' he said.

'Okay.' Mahon put the receiver down.

'Got to get on with it now, Nancy,' he said. He told her what he'd heard from Mahon.

He settled himself at his desk and began work again, making notes and equations on the pad beside him. Tomorrow he would have to go back to the centre and use the computers himself.

As he worked, Nancy kept him supplied with coffee and snacks. By eight the next morning he began to feel he was getting somewhere. He assembled his notes, put them in a folder, and was about to say goodbye to Nancy when she said:

'Mind if I come along, Fusty. I wouldn't like to have to hang around here for you again.'

'Okay,' he said. 'Let's go.'

As they arrived at The Golden Gate they found that the place had a visitor. It was Gordon Ogg. He came forward with John Mahon, through a confusion of technicians and machinery that now filled the dance hall.

'Mr Ogg wants to see you, professor,' Mahon said. 'He's got some news about Orelli, I think.'

'We'd better go upstairs, Gordon,' Faustaff said. They climbed the staircase to the second floor and entered a small, cluttered room where old furniture had been piled. 'This'll have to do,' Faustaff said as they sat down where they could. Nancy was still with them. Faustaff didn't feel like asking her to wait anywhere else.

'I must apologise for leaving you behind on E-11.' Ogg stroked his long moustache, looking even more mournful than usual. 'But then I had no conception of what was going on. You know it all, I suppose— the destruction of E-14 and E-13, the war that is destroying E-1?'

'Yes.' Faustaff nodded.

'And you know that Orelli has leagued himself with this chap with a funny name . . . ?'

'Steifflomeis. I suspected it. Though I'm still unable to think what mutual interest they have. It is in yours and Orelli's for things to remain basically unchanged.'

'As salvagers, yes. But Orelli has other schemes. That's why I came to see you. He contacted me this morning, at my base on E-2.'

'So he is alive. I thought so.'

'This other chap—Steifflomeis—was with him. They wanted my help. From what I can gather Steifflomeis was working for another group, but he's turned traitor. That was a little obscure. I couldn't

119

quite make out who the other group were. There's a new parallel been formed, I gather . . .'

'E-Zero, that's right. Did they tell you anything about it?'

'Nothing much. Steifflomeis said something about its not having been "activated" yet, whatever that means. Anyway they have plans for going there and setting up their own government, something like that. Orelli was cautious, he didn't tell me much. He concentrated mainly on telling me that all the other worlds are due to break up soon and nothing will be able to stop this happening, that I might just as well throw in my lot with him and Steifflomeis since I had everything to lose and something to gain. I told him that I wasn't interested.'

'Why did you do that?'

'Call it a psychological quirk. As you know, professor, I have never felt any malice towards you and have always been careful never to attack you or any of your men by using violence. I preferred to leave you and work on my own—that's part of the same psychological quirk. But now it looks as if the crunch is coming, I wondered if I could help.'

Faustaff was touched by Ogg's statement. 'I am sure you could. Just the act of offering has helped me, Gordon. I suppose you have no idea how Orelli and Steifflomeis intend to get through to E-Zero?'

'Not really. They did refer to E-3 at one point, I think they might have had some equipment here. They certainly boasted of a refined tunneller— Steifflomeis seemed to link it with a disrupter that Orelli had captured. They can shift much bigger masses through subspace, I gathered.'

120

'So that's what happened to the cathedral. But where is it now?'

'The cathedral?'

Faustaff explained. Ogg said he knew nothing of this.

'I have the feeling,' Faustaff said, 'that the shifting of the cathedral has no real significance. It would have been done simply to exhibit the power of the new tunneller. But it is difficult to see why Steifflomeis has reneged on his own people. I'd better fill you in on this.' He repeated all he knew about Steifflomeis and Maggy White.

Ogg took all the information expressionlessly. 'An alien race manipulating human beings from somewhere beyond Earth. It sounds too fantastic, professor. Yet I'm convinced.'

'I think I've been foolish,' Faustaff said. 'You say they mentioned a base on E-3. We know about it. There might be a chance of finding something after all. Do you want to come and see, Gordon?'

'If you'd like me along.'

'I would. Come on.'

The three of them left the room. Faustaff enquired about air transport, but there was none available. He did not dare wait on the off-chance of a 'copter coming through and he was not sure enough of himself to requisition one being used for evacuation purposes. He got into his Buick and they drove out of San Francisco, heading for Los Angeles.

They looked a strange trio, Faustaff driving; his huge body squeezed into the inadequate seat of the car, Nancy and Ogg in the back seats. Ogg had insisted on bringing the antiquated machine-gun he always carried. His tall, thin body was held erect, the gun cradled in his arm. He looked like a Victorian nobleman on safari, his eyes staring straight ahead down the long road that stretched into the Great American Desert.

11

The Way Through

They found the house that had been marked for them on their map by Mahon before they left.

It lay in a quiet Beverley Hills cul-de-sac about fifty yards from the road. A well-kept lawn lay in front and a gravel drive led to the house. They drove up it. Faustaff was too tired to bother about secrecy. They got out of the car and a couple of heaves of Faustaff's body broke the door open. They moved into the hall. It was wide and an open staircase led up from it.

'Mahon said they'd found the equipment in the back room,' Faustaff said, leading the way there. He opened the door. Orelli stood there. He was alone, but his rifle was pointing straight at Faustaff's head. His thin lips smiled.

'Professor Faustaff. We'd missed you.'

'Forget the villainous dialogue, Orelli.' Faustaff skipped suddenly to one side and rushed at the ex-cardinal who pulled the trigger. A beam went high and pierced the outer wall. Faustaff began to grapple the gun from Orelli who was now snarling.

Orelli plainly hadn't expected such sudden action from Faustaff who was normally loathe to indulge in any sort of violence.

Ogg stepped in behind him while Nancy hovered in the doorway. He pushed the muzzle of his machine gun into Orelli's back and said softly: 'I shall have to kill you unless you are sensible, Orelli. Drop your rifle.'

'Turncoat!' Orelli said as he dropped the gun. He seemed offended and surprised by Ogg's allying himself with Faustaff. 'Why have you sided with this fool?'

Ogg didn't bother to reply. He tugged the laser rifle's cord from the power pack on Orelli's back and threw the gun across the room.

'Where's Steifflomeis and the rest of your men, Orelli?' Faustaff asked. 'We're impatient—we want to know a lot quickly. We're ready to kill you unless you tell us.'

'Steifflomeis and my men are on the new planet.'

'E-Zero? How did you get through when we couldn't?'

'Steifflomeis has far greater resources than yours, professor. You were stupid to offend him. A man with his knowledge is worth cultivating.'

'I wasn't interested in cultivating him, I was more interested in stopping him from killing me, if you remember.'

Orelli turned to Ogg. 'And you, Gordon, taking sides against me, a fellow salvager. I am disappointed.'

'We have nothing in common, Orelli. Answer the professor's questions.'

Just then Nancy shouted and pointed. Turning, Faustaff saw that the air behind him seemed to glow and the wall beyond became hazy. A tunnel was being formed. Steifflomeis must be coming through.

He picked up the useless laser rifle and stood watching the tunnel as it shimmered and took shape. It was of a glowing reddish colour, unlike the dull grey of the tunnels he was used to. Out of it stepped Steifflomeis, he was unarmed. He smiled, apparently unperturbed, when he saw what had happened.

'What are you trying to do, professor?' Behind him the tunnel began to fade.

'We're after information primarily, Herr Steifflomeis,' Faustaff answered, feeling more confident now that it was plain Steifflomeis had no more men with him. 'Are you going to give it to us here, or must we take you back to our headquarters?'

'What sort of information, Professor Faustaff?'

'Firstly we want to know how you can get through to E-Zero when we can't.'

'Better machines, professor.'

'Who made the machines?'

'My erstwhile principals. I could not tell you how to build one, only how to work one.'

'Well, you can show us.'

'If you wish.' Steifflomeis shrugged and went to a machine that was evidently the main console for the rest of the devices in the room. 'It is a simple matter of tapping out a set of co-ordinates and setting a switch.'

Faustaff decided that Steifflomeis was probably telling the truth and he didn't know how the advanced tunneller worked. He would have to get a team down here immediately and have them check it over.

'Can you keep them covered, Gordon?' he said.

'I'll phone my headquarters and get some people here as soon as possible.'

Ogg nodded and Faustaff went into the hall where he'd seen the phone.

He got through to the operator and gave her the number he wanted. The phone rang for some time before someone answered. He asked for Mahon.

At length Mahon came on the line and Faustaff told him what had happened. Mahon promised to send a team up by 'copter right away.

Faustaff was just going back into the room when he heard footsteps on the path outside. He went to the door and there was Maggy White.

'Professor Faustaff,' she nodded, as seemingly unsurprised by his presence as Steifflomeis had been. Faustaff began to think that all his recent actions had been anticipated.

'Were you expecting me to be here?' he asked.

'No. Is Steifflomeis here?'

'He is.'

'Where?'

'In the back room. You'd better join him.'

She went ahead of Faustaff, looked at Nancy curiously and then stepped into the room.

'We've got them all now,' Faustaff said, feeling much better. 'We'll wait for the team to arrive and then we can get down to business. I suppose,' he turned to Steifflomeis, 'you or Miss White wouldn't like to tell us the whole story before they come?'

'I might,' Steifflomeis said, 'particularly since it would now be best if I convinced you to throw in your lot with Cardinal Orelli and myself.'

Faustaff glanced at Maggy White. 'Do you feel the

same as Steifflomeis? Are you prepared to tell me more?'

She shook her head. 'And I shouldn't believe too much of what he tells you, either, professor.'

Steifflomeis glanced at his wrist watch.

'It doesn't matter now,' he said, almost cheerfully. 'We appear to be on our way.'

Suddenly it seemed that the whole house was lifted by a whirlwind and Faustaff thought briefly that Orelli had rightly called him a fool. He should have realised that what could be done with a gigantic cathedral could also be done with a small house.

The sensation of movement was brief, but the scene through the window was very different. Amorphous, it gave the impression of an unfinished painted stage set. Trees and hedges were there, the sky, sunlight, but none of them seemed real.

'Well, you wanted to get here, professor,' smiled Steifflomeis, 'and here we are. I think you called it E-Zero.'

12

The Petrified Place

Maggy White glowered at Steifflomeis who seemed very full of himself at that moment.

'What do you think you're doing?' she said harshly. 'This goes against . . .'

'I don't care,' Steifflomeis shrugged. 'If Faustaff could get away with so much, then so can I—we, if you like.' He turned a light-hearted eye on Faustaff who had still not completely recovered from the shock of transition between E-3 and E-Zero.

'Well, professor,' Faustaff heard Steifflomeis say. 'Are you impressed?'

'I'm curious,' said Faustaff slowly.

Orelli began to chuckle and moved towards Faustaff, but was stopped short by Ogg's now somewhat nervous gun nudging at him. Ogg's expression had become resolute, but he seemed baffled. Nancy looked rather the same.

Orelli said sharply: 'Gordon! Put the gun away. That was a silly gesture. We are in the position of power now, no matter how many guns you point at us. You realise that? You must!'

Faustaff pulled himself together. 'What if we order you to return us to E-3? We could kill you if you refused.'

'I am not so sure you would kill us, professor,' Steifflomeis smiled. 'And in any case it takes hours to prepare for a transition. We would need technical help too. All our people are at the cathedral.' He pointed out of the window to where a spire could be seen over the tops of roofs and trees. The spire seemed unnaturally solid in the peculiarly unreal setting. Part of the impression was gained, Fausta realised, by the fact that the whole landscape, aside from the spire, looked unused. 'Also,' Steifflomeis continued, 'they are expecting us and will come here soon if we do not turn up there.'

'We still have you,' Ogg reminded him. 'We can barter your lives for a safe transport back to where we came from.'

'You could,' Steifflomeis admitted. 'But what would that gain you? Isn't E-Zero where you wanted to come?' He glanced at Faustaff. 'That's true isn't it, professor?'

Faustaff nodded.

'You will have to be careful here, professor,' Orelli put in. 'I am serious. You had better throw in with us. United we stand, eh?'

'I prefer to stay divided, particularly if you fall as well,' Faustaff replied dryly.

'This antagonism is unrealistic, professor. Cut your losses.' Steifflomeis looked somewhat nervously out of the window. 'The potential danger here is great; this is an unactivated simulation—it's delicate. A few wrong moves on your part would, among other things, make it almost impossible to return to any one of the other simulations ...'

'Simulations of what?' said Faustaff, still trying

to get concrete information from Steifflomeis.

'The original . . .'

'Steifflomeis!' Maggy White broke in. 'What are you doing? The principals might easily decide to re-call us!'

Steifflomeis responded coolly. 'How will they reach us?' he asked her. 'We are the most sophisticated agents they have.'

'They can recall you—you know that.'

'Not easily—not without some co-operation from me. They will never succeed with the simulations. They have tried too many times and failed too many times. With our knowledge we can resist them —we can become independent—live our own lives. We can leave this world only semi-activated and rule it. There would be nothing to stop us.'

Maggy White lunged towards Ogg and tried to grab the machine-gun from him. He backed away. Faustaff got hold of the woman, but she already had both hands on the gun. Suddenly the gun went off. It had been set to semi-automatic. A stream of bullets smashed through the window.

'Careful!' shrieked Steifflomeis.

As if startled by the firing, Maggy White took her hands away. Orelli had moved towards Ogg, but the tall Englishman turned the gun on him again and he stopped.

Steifflomeis was staring out of the window.

Faustaff looked in the same direction, and saw that where the bullets had struck the nearest house its walls were falling. One had cracked and was crumbling, but the others fell neatly down, to lie on the ground in one piece. The impression of a stage-set was retained—yet the walls, and the revealed interior of the house, which was now falling slowly, were evidently quite solid and real.

Steifflomeis turned on Maggy.

'You accuse me—and cause that to happen,' he said, pointing out at the wreckage. 'I suppose you were going to try to kill me.'

'I still intend to.'

Steifflomeis swung the pointing finger at Faustaff. 'There is the one you should kill. One of us should have done it long since.'

'I am not so sure now,' she said. 'He might even be of use to the principals. Not you, though.'

'No indeed,' smiled Steifflomeis, lowering his arm. 'You realise what your action might have started?'

She nodded. 'And that wouldn't be to your advantage, would it, Steifflomeis?'

'It would be to no-one's advantage,' Steifflomeis said, rubbing his eyes. 'And it would be very unpleasant for Faustaff and the others—including you, Orelli, as I've explained.'

Orelli smiled to himself. It was a wickedly introspective smile as if he looked into his own soul and was pleased with the evil he found there. He leant against one of the pieces of machinery and folded his arms. 'What you told me sounds almost attractive, Steifflomeis.'

Faustaff became impatient. He felt that he should be taking some sort of action but he could think of nothing to do.

'We'll pay a visit to the cathedral I think,' he said on impulse. 'Let's get going.'

Steifflomeis was plainly aware of Faustaff's uncer-

131

tainty. He did not move as Ogg waved the gun towards the door.

'Why would the cathedral be better, Professor Faustaff?' he asked lightly. 'After all, there are more of our men there.'

'True,' Faustaff answered. 'But we might just as well go. I've made up my mind, Steifflomeis. Move, please.' His tone was unusually firm. Hearing it, he was not sure that he liked it. Was he compromising himself too much? he wondered.

Steifflomeis shrugged and walked past Ogg towards the door. Orelli was already opening it. Maggy White and Nancy followed Ogg with Faustaff keeping an eye on Maggy.

They went out into the hall and Orelli pulled the front door wide.

The lawn and gravel path looked only slightly different from what they had left on E-3. Yet there was something hazy about them, something unformed. Faustaff thought that the feeling they aroused was familiar and as they began to walk down the path towards the street he realised that, for all their apparent reality, they had the effect of making him feel as if he were experiencing a particularly naturalistic dream.

The effect was made perfect by the stillness of the air, the complete silence everywhere. Though he could feel the gravel beneath his feet, he made no sound as he walked.

Even when he spoke, his voice seemed so distant that he had the impression its sound carried around the whole planet before it reached his ears.

'Does that street lead to the cathedral?' he asked

132

Steifflomeis, pointing to the street at the bottom of the lawn.

Steifflomeis's lips were tight. His eyes seemed to express some kind of warning as he turned and nodded at Faustaff.

Orelli appeared more relaxed. He also turned his head while he walked jauntily towards the street. 'That's the one, professor,' he said. His voice sounded far away, too, although it was perfectly audible.

Steifflomeis looked nervously at his partner. To Faustaff it seemed that Steifflomeis was privately wondering if he had made a mistake in joining forces with Orelli. Faustaff had known Orelli much longer than Steifflomeis and was well aware that the ex-cardinal was at best a treacherous and neurotic ally, given to moods that seemed to indicate a strong death-wish and which led him and anyone associated with him into unnecessary danger.

Wanting something to happen, something he could at least try to deal with, Faustaff almost welcomed Orelli's mood.

They reached the street. Cars were parked there. They were new and Faustaff recognised them as the latest on E-1. Evidently, whoever created these 'simulations' didn't start from scratch.

There was no-one about. E-Zero seemed unpopulated. Nothing lived. Even the trees and plants gave the impression of lifelessness.

Orelli stopped and waved his arms shouting. 'They're here, professor! They must have heard the shots. What are you going to do now?'

Turning a corner came about a dozen of Orelli's brigandly gang, their laser-rifles ready in their hands.

Faustaff bellowed: 'Stop! We've got Steifflomeis and Orelli covered!' He felt a bit self-conscious, then, and looked at Ogg, feeling he was better able to take the initiative.

Ogg said nothing but he straddled his legs slightly and moved his machine gun a little. His expression was abnormally stern. Orelli's men stopped.

'What are you going to do now Faustaff?' Orelli repeated.

Faustaff glanced at Ogg again but Ogg apparently refused to meet his gaze. There was a big hovercar close by. Faustaff contemplated it.

Steifflomeis said softly: 'It would be unwise to do anything with the automobile. Please professor, don't use any of the things you find here.'

'Why not?' Faustaff asked in the same tone.

'To do so could trigger a sequence of events that would snowball until nobody could control them. I'm speaking the truth. There is a ritual involved— every simulation has its ritual before it becomes completely activated. The gun going off doesn't appear to have had any result—but starting a car could begin the initial awakening . . .'

'I'll kill him if you come any closer!'

Ogg was talking to Orelli's men who had begun to stir. He was pointing the gun directly at Orelli, Steifflomeis apparently forgotten. The normally stoical Ogg now seemed to be under stress. He must have hated Orelli for a long time, Faustaff reflected. Or perhaps he hated what Orelli represented in himself. It was quite plain to them all that Ogg hoped to kill Orelli.

Only Orelli himself seemed relaxed, grinning at Ogg. Ogg frowned now, sweating. His hands shook.

'Gordon!' Faustaff said desperately. 'If you kill him, they'll start shooting.'

'I know,' Ogg replied, and his eyes narrowed.

Behind them Maggy White had started to run up the road, away from Orelli's men. Steifflomeis was the only one to turn his head and watch her, his face thoughtful.

Faustaff decided to go to the car. He gripped the door handle. He pressed the button and the door opened. He noticed that the keys were in the ignition. 'Keep them covered Gordon,' he said as he got into the driving seat. 'Come on, Nancy.'

Nancy followed him, sitting next to him.

'Gordon!' he called. He started the engine. He realised that he hadn't considered the possibility that the car wouldn't work. The motor began to turn over.

Faustaff called to Ogg again and was relieved to see that he was edging towards the car. Nancy opened the back door for him and he slid in. His gun was still pointing directly at Orelli.

Faustaff touched a button. The car rose on its air-cushion and they began to move down the road, slowly at first.

One shot came from a laser rifle. The beam went high.

Faustaff put his foot down, hearing Steifflomeis order the men to stop firing.

'Faustaff!' Steifflomeis yelled, and although they

were now some distance away he could hear him perfectly. 'Faustaff—you and your friends will suffer most from this!'

They passed Maggy White on the way, but they didn't stop for her.

13

The Time Dump

As Faustaff drove into downtown Los Angeles he
realised that everything was not as normal as he had
thought. Much of the area was unfinished, as if work
on the 'simulation' had been abandoned or interrupted. Houses were intact, stores bore familiar signs
—but every so often he would pass something that
clashed with the effect.

A tree in a garden, for instance, was recognisable
as a Baiera tree with sparse, primitive foliage. The
tree had flourished during the Jurassic, up to 180
million years in the past. A block that Faustaff remembered as having once been taken up with a big
movie theatre was now a vacant lot. On it were
pitched Indian wigwams reminiscent of those that
had been used by the Western plains Indians. The
whole appearance of the settlement did not give the
impression of its having been built as an exhibit.
Elsewhere were wooden houses of a style typical of
three centuries earlier, a brand new 1908 Model T
Ford with gleaming black enamel, brass fittings, and
wheel-spokes picked out in red. A store window dis-
played women's fashions of almost two hundred
years before.

Although, in general appearance, the city was the modern Los Angeles of 1999 on E-1, the anachronisms were plentiful and easily noticed standing out in sharp contrast to everything else. They added to Faustaff's impression that he was dreaming. He began to experience vague feelings of fear and he drove the car away very fast, heading towards Hollywood for no other reason than because that was where the highway was leading him.

Nancy Hunt gripped his arm. Evidently close to hysteria herself, she tried to comfort him. 'Don't worry, Fusty,' she said. 'We'll get out of this. I can't even believe it's real.'

'It's real enough,' he said, relaxing a little. 'Or at least the threat is. You just can't—I don't know—get to grips with the place. There's something basically intangible about it—the houses, the street, the scenery—it isn't one thing or another.' He addressed Gordon Ogg who was still grim-faced, hugging his machine gun to him, eyes hooded.

'How do you feel, Gordon?'

Ogg moved in his seat and looked directly at Faustaff whose head was half-turned towards him. Faustaff saw that there were tears in Ogg's eyes.

'Uncomfortable,' Ogg replied with some effort. 'It's not just the scenery—it's me. I can't seem to control my emotions—or my mind. I feel that this world isn't so much unreal as . . .' he paused. 'It's a different quality of reality, perhaps. We are unreal to *it*—we shouldn't be here. Even if we had a right to be here, we shouldn't be behaving as we are. It's our state of mind, if you like. That's what's wrong—our state of mind, not the place.'

138

Faustaff nodded thoughtfully. 'But do you think you'd be willing to enter the state of mind you feel this world demands?'

Ogg hesitated. Then he said: 'No I don't think so.'

'Then I know what you mean,' Faustaff went on. 'I'm going through the same thing. We've got to try to hang on, Gordon—this world wants us to alter our identities. Do you want to alter your identity?'

'No.'

'Do you mean personality?' Nancy asked. 'That's the feeling I've got—that at any moment if I relaxed enough I just wouldn't be me any more. It's like dying, almost. A sort of dying. I feel that something of me would be left but it would be—naked . . .'

Their attempts to express and analyse their fears had not helped. Now the atmosphere in the car was one of terror—they had brought their fears to the surface and they were unable to control them.

The car rushed down the highway, carrying a frightened cargo. Above them, the featureless sky added to their impression that time and space as they knew it no longer existed, that they no longer possessed a fragment of potential influence over their situation.

Faustaff tried to speak again, to suggest that perhaps after all they should turn round and throw themselves on Steifflomeis's mercy, that he at least would have an explanation of what was happening to them, that they might accept his suggestion of their combining forces with him until they saw an opportunity of escaping from E-Zero.

The words that came out of his mouth held no

meaning for him. The other two did not hear him, it seemed.

Faustaff's large hands shook violently on the steering wheel. He barely resisted the urge to let the car crash.

He drove on a while longer and then, with a feeling of hopelessness, stopped the car suddenly. He leaned over the steering wheel, his face contorted, his mouth gibbering while another part of his mind sought the core of sanity that must still be within him and which might help him resist the identity-sapping influence of E-Zero.

Did he want to resist? The question kept entering his mind. At length, in trying to answer, he recovered partial sanity. Yes, he did—at least, until he understood what he was resisting.

He looked up. There were no houses in the immediate vicinity. There were some seen in the distance behind and ahead of him, but here the highway went across sparse grassland. It looked like a site that had been levelled for development and then left. What caught his eye, however, was the dump.

At first glance it looked like a garbage dump, a huge hill of miscellaneous junk.

Then Faustaff realised that it wasn't junk. All the objects looked new and whole.

On impulse he got out of the car and began to work towards the vast heap.

As he got closer he could see that it was even bigger than he had first thought. It rose at least a hundred feet above him. He saw a complete Greek Winged Victory in marble; a seventeenth century arquebus, gleaming oak, brass and iron; a large Chinese kite painted with a dragon's head in brilliant primary colours. A Fokker Triplane of the type used in the 1914–18 war lay close to the top, its wood and canvas as new as the day it left its factory. There were wagon wheels and what looked like an Egyptian boat; a throne that might have belonged to a Byzantine Emperor; a big Victorian urn bearing a heavy floral pattern; an Indian elephant howdah; a stuffed Timber Wolf; a sixteenth century arbalest—a crossbow made of steel; a late eighteenth century electric generator; a set of Japanesee horse armour on a beautifully carved wooden horse, and a North African drum; a life-sized bronze statue of a Sinhalese woman; a Scandinavian rune stone and a Babylonian obelisk.

All history seemed to have been piled together at random. It was a mountain of treasure, as if some mad museum curator had found a way of up-ending his museum and shaking its contents out on to the ground. Yet the artifacts did not have the look of museum-pieces. Everything looked absolutely new.

Faustaff approached the heap until he stood immediately beneath it. At his feet lay a near-oval shield of wood and leather. It looked as if it belonged to the fourteenth century and the workmanship seemed Italian. It was richly decorated with gold and red paint and its main motif showed an ornate mythical lion; beside it, on its side, was a beautiful clock dating from around 1700. It was of steel and silver filigree and might have been the work of the greatest clockmaker of his time, Thomas Tompion. Few other craftsmen, Faustaff thought abstractedly, could have created such a clock. Quite close to the clock he saw a skull of blue crystal. It could only have been fifteenth century Aztec. Faustaff had seen one like it in the British Museum. Half-covering the crystal skull was a grotesque ceremonial mask that looked as if it came from New Guinea, the features painted to represent a devil.

Faustaff felt overwhelmed by the richness and beauty—and the sheer variety—of the jumble of objects. Somehow it represented an aspect of what he had been fighting for since he had taken over the organisation from his father and agreed to try to preserve the worlds of subspace.

He reached down and picked up the heavy Tompion clock, running his fingers over the ornate silver. A key hung by a red cord from the back. He opened the glass door at the front and inserted the key. Smoothly the key turned and he started to wind the clock. Inside a balance wheel began to swing with a muted tick-tock. Faustaff set the hands to twelve o'clock and, holding the clock carefully, put it down.

Although the sense of unreality about his surroundings was still strong, this action had helped him. He squatted in front of the clock and tried to think, his back to the great mound of antiques.

He concentrated his whole attention on the clock as, with an effort, he considered what he knew about E-Zero.

It was fairly obvious that E-Zero was simply the latest 'simulation' created by whoever had employed Steifflomeis, Maggy White and the D-squaders. It was also almost certain that this simulation was no different from what the other thousand had been like

at the same stage. His own world, E-1, must therefore have been created in the same way, its history
beginning at the point where E-2's history had become static. That would mean that E-1 had been created in the early sixties, shortly before his own birth,
but certainly not before his father's birth—and his
father had discovered the alternate worlds in 1971.
It was unpleasant to consider that his father, and
many of the people he had known and some of whom
he still knew, must have been 'activated' on a world
that had originally been a world like E-Zero. Had
the inhabitants of his own world been transported
from one subspacial world to another? If so, how
had they been conditioned into accepting their new
environment? There was no explanation as he wondered again why the inhabitants of all the worlds
other than E-1 accepted without question the
changes in their society and their geography result-
ing from a series of Unstable Matter Situations? He
had often wondered about it. He had once described
them as seeming to live in a perpetual dream and a
perpetual present.

The difference on E-Zero was that *he* felt real
enough, but the whole planet seemed to be a dream-
world also in a state of static time. For all the bizarre
changes that had taken place on the other subspacial
worlds, he had never got this impression from them
—only from the inhabitants.

Evidently the conditioning that occurred on the
drastically altered worlds would be applied more or
less in reverse on E-Zero.

He could not consider who had created the alternate Earths. He would have to hope that at some

time he would be able to get the answers once and for all, from either Maggy White or Steifflomeis. He could not even guess why the worlds had been created and then destroyed. The kind of science necessary for such a task would be far too sophisticated for him to comprehend immediately, even if he never learned its principles.

The creators of the subspacial worlds seemed unable to interfere with them directly. That was why they had created the android D-squaders, obviously —to destroy their work. Steifflomeis and Maggy White had made a more recent appearance. Plainly, they were either human or robots of a much more advanced type than the D-squaders and their job was not directly concerned with demolishing the subspacial Earths but with eliminating random factors like himself.

Therefore the creators, whoever and wherever they were, were not able to control their creations completely. The inhabitants of the worlds must have a fair degree of free will, otherwise he and his father would never have been able to set up the organisation they had used to preserve and bring relief to the other alternates. The creators, in short, were by no means omnipotent—they were not even omniscient, otherwise they would have acted sooner than they had in sending Steifflomeis and Maggy White in to get rid of him. That was encouraging, at least. It was obvious, too, that Steifflomeis believed they could be disobeyed, for Steifflomeis had plainly reneged on them and was out to oppose them. Whether or not this opposition would succeed Faustaff could not tell since only Steifflomeis and Maggy

White knew exactly what was opposed. Maggy White was still loyal. Perhaps she had some way of contracting her 'principals' and had already warned them of Steifflomeis's treachery. Steifflomeis hadn't appeared to be worried by this possibility. Could these principals be relying solely on Steifflomeis and Maggy White? Why, if that were the case, were they so powerful and at the same time so powerless? Another question he could not yet begin to answer.

Faustaff remembered that he had recently considered temporarily taking Steifflomeis up on his offer. Now he rejected the idea. Steifflomeis and Orelli had both proved untrustworthy—Steifflomeis to his employers, Orelli to him. But Maggy White seemed loyal to her principals and she had once said that Faustaff's ideals and theirs were not so different in the long-term.

Maggy White then, must be found. If he were going to seek anyone's help—and it was evident that he must—then she was the one. There was a strong possibility, of course, that she had now left E-Zero or been captured by Steifflomeis.

All that he could hope for now, he thought, would be a chance of contacting the creators. Then at least he would know exactly what he fought. Perhaps Maggy White could be convinced. Hadn't she said to Steifflomeis that he, Faustaff, would be of more use to her principals than Steifflomeis now? Faustaff had failed to thwart them, but he could still hope to find a way of convincing them of the immorality of their actions.

He had no idea where Maggy had gone. The only course open to him was to retrace his journey and

145

see if he could find her.

All this time he had been staring at the clock, but now he noticed the position of the hands; exactly an hour had passed. He got to his feet and picked up the clock.

Looking about him he still felt disturbed by the continuing unreality of his surroundings; but he felt less confused by them, less at their mercy.

He began to walk back towards the car.

It was only when he had reached it and climbed in that he realised Nancy Hunt and Gordon Ogg were no longer there.

He looked in all directions, hoping that he would see them; but they were gone.

Had they been captured by Steifflomeis and Orelli? Had Maggy White found them and forced them to go with her? Or had they simply fled, totally demoralised by their fear?

Now there was an additional reason for finding Maggy White as soon as possible.

14

The Crucifixion in the Cathedral

As he drove back down the highway, seeing the spires of the cathedral over the roofs of the houses ahead, Faustaff wished that he had brought one of the guns he had seen on the dump. He would have felt better for possessing a weapon of some kind.

He slowed the car suddenly as he saw some figures approaching him down the middle of the highway. They were behaving in a peculiar way and seemed oblivious to his car.

When he got closer he recognised them as Orelli's men, but differently dressed. They wore unfamiliar, festive costumes of the kind normally seen at carnivals. Some were dressed as Roman soldiers; some, he gathered, as priests, and others as women. They came down the highway performing an exaggerated high-stepping walk and they wore rapt, uncomprehending expressions.

Faustaff felt no fear of them and sounded the car's horn. They did not appear to hear it. Very slowly, he drove the car around them, looking at them as closely as he could. There was something familiar about the costumes; what they represented struck a chord in him, but he could not analyse what it was, and he did not feel he had the time to work it out.

He passed them and then passed the house in which he'd been transported to E-Zero. The house still looked much more real in contrast to the others near it. He turned a bend in the street and saw the cathedral ahead. It was in its own grounds, surrounded by a stone wall. Let into the wall were two solid gate-posts and the big wrought-iron gates were open. He drove straight through them. He felt that caution would be useless.

He stopped the car at the west-front of the cathedral where the main entrance lay, flanked by tall towers. Like most cathedrals, this one seemed to have been built and rebuilt over several centuries though in general appearance it was Gothic, with the unmistakable arches of its stained-glass windows and heavy, iron-studded doors.

Faustaff mounted the few steps until he stood at the doors. They were slightly ajar and he pushed them partially open, just enough for him to pass through. He walked into the nave, the vast ceiling rising above him, and it was as empty of seats as it had been when he had last been in it. But the altar was there now, and candles burned on it. It was covered by an exquisite altar cloth. Faustaff barely noticed these, for it was the life-size crucifix behind the altar which drew his attention. Not only was it life-size but peculiarly life-like, also. Faustaff walked rapidly towards it, refusing to believe what he already knew to be true.

The cross was of plain wood, though well-finished. The figure nailed to it was alive.

It was Orelli, naked and bleeding from wounds

148

in his hands and feet, his chest rising and falling rapidly, his head hanging on his chest.

Now Faustaff realised what Orelli's men had represented—the people of Calvary. They must certainly have been the ones who crucified him.

With a grunt of horror Faustaff ran forward and climbed on the altar reaching up to see how he could get Orelli down. The ex-cardinal smelled of sweat and his body was lacerated. On his head was a thorn garland.

What had caused Orelli's men to do this to him? It was surely no conscious perversion of Christianity; no deliberate blasphemy. Faustaff doubted that Orelli's brigands cared enough for religion to do what they had done.

He would need something to lever the nails out.

Then Orelli raised his head and opened his eyes.

Faustaff was shocked by the tranquillity he saw in those eyes. Orelli's whole face seemed transformed not into a travesty of Christ but into a living representation of Christ.

Orelli smiled sweetly at Faustaff. 'Can I help you, my son?' he said calmly.

'Orelli?' Faustaff was unable to say anything else for a moment. He paused. 'How did this happen?' he asked eventually.

'It was my destiny,' Orelli replied. 'I knew it and they understood what they must do. I must die, you see.'

'This is insane!' Faustaff began trying to tug at one of the nails. 'You aren't Christ! What's happening?'

'What must happen,' Orelli said in the same even

149

tone. 'Go away, my son. Do not question this. Leave me.'

'But you're Orelli—a traitor, murderer, renegade. You—you don't deserve this! You've no right . . .' Faustaff was an atheist and to him Christianity was one of many religions that had ceased to serve any purpose, but something in the spectacle before him disturbed him. 'The Christ in the Bible was an idea, not a man!' he shouted. 'You've turned it inside out!'

'We are all ideas,' Orelli replied, 'either our own or someone else's. I am an idea in their minds and I am the same idea in my own. What has happened is true—it is real—it is necessary! Do not try to help me. I don't need any help.'

Though he spoke distantly, Faustaff had the impression that Orelli also spoke with preternatural lucidity. It gave him some insight into what he feared on E-Zero. The world not only threatened to destroy the personality—it turned a man inside out. Orelli's outer *persona* was buried within him somewhere (if he had not lost it altogether) and here was revealed his innermost self; not the Devil he had tried to be but the Christ he had wanted to be.

Slowly, Faustaff got down from the altar while Orelli's calm face smiled at him. It was no idiot's smile, it was not insane—it was a smile of fulfilment. Its sanity and tranquillity terrified Faustaff. He turned his back on it and began to walk with effort towards the door.

As he neared it a figure stepped out from the shadows of the arches and touched his arm.

'Orelli does not only die for you, professor,'

150

Steifflomeis said smiling. 'He dies because of you. You began the activation. I compliment you on your strength of will. I should have expected you to have succumbed by now. All the others have.'

'Succumbed to what exactly, Steifflomeis?'

'To the Ritual—the Activation Ritual. Every new planet must undergo it. Under normal circumstances the entire population of a fresh simulation must play out its myth rôles before it awakes. "The work before the dream and the dream before the wakening", as some writer of yours once put it. You people have some reasonable insights into your situation from time to time, you know. Come.' Steifflomeis led Faustaff from the cathedral, 'I can take you to see more. The show is about to start in earnest. I can't guarantee that you will survive it.'

A sun now shone in the sky, bringing bright lights and heavy shade to the world, though it still did not live. The sun was swollen and a glowing red; Faustaff blinked and reached into his pocket to get his sunglasses. He put them on.

'That's right,' grinned Steifflomeis. 'Gird on your armour and prepare for an interesting battle.'

'Where are we going?' Faustaff asked vaguely.

'Out into the world. You will see it naked. Every man has his rôle to play today. You have defeated me, Faustaff—perhaps you had not realised that. You have set E-Zero in motion by your ignorant actions. I can only hope that E-Zero will defeat you in turn, though I am not sure.'

'Why aren't you sure?' Faustaff asked, still only half-interested.

'There are levels that even I had not prepared for,'

Steifflomeis answered. 'Perhaps you will not find your rôle on E-Zero. Perhaps you have resisted and retained your personality because you are already living your rôle. Could it be that we have all under-estimated you?'

15

The Revels of E-Zero

Faustaff could not understand the full implication of Steifflomeis's statement but he allowed the man to lead him out of the cathedral grounds and into a wooded park behind it.

'You know there is little left of E-1 now,' Steifflomeis said casually as they walked. 'The war was very brief. I think a few survivors are lingering on, by all accounts.'

Faustaff knew that Steifflomeis had deliberately chosen this moment to tell him, probably hoping to demoralise him. He controlled the feelings of loss and despair that came to him and tried to answer as casually.

'It was only to be expected, I suppose.'

Steifflomeis smiled. 'You might be pleased to know that many people from the other simulations have been transferred to E-Zero. Not an act of mercy on the part of the principals, of course. Merely a selection of the most likely specimens for populating this Earth.'

Faustaff paused. Ahead he could make out a number of figures. He peered through the trees at them, frowning. Most of them were naked. Like Orelli's men, they were moving in a ritualistic, puppet-like manner, their faces blank. There was an approximately equal number of men and women.

Steifflomeis waved a hand. 'They will not see us— we are invisible to them while they are in this state.'

Faustaff was fascinated. 'What are they doing?'

'Oh, working out their positions in the world. We'll go a little closer, if you like.'

Steifflomeis led Faustaff towards the group.

Faustaff felt he was witnessing an ancient and primitive ceremony. People seemed to be imitating animals of various kinds. One man had branches tied to his head in a familiar representation of a stag. A combination of man, beast and plant which was significant to Faustaff without his understanding quite why. A woman stooped and picked up the skin of a lioness draping it around her naked body. There was a pile of animal skins in the centre of the posturing group. Some of the people already wore skins or masks. Here were representations of bears, owls, hares, wolves, snakes, eagles, bats, foxes, badgers and many other animals. A fire burned to one side of the glade.

Soon the whole group had clothed itself in pelts or masks.

In the centre now stood a woman. She wore a dog's skin around her shoulders and a crudely painted dog's mask on her face. She had long black hair that escaped from behind the mask and fell down her back. The dance around her became increasingly formal, but much faster than previously.

Faustaff grew tense as he watched.

The circle drew tighter and tighter around the dogwoman. She stood there impassively until the

154

group suddenly stopped and faced her. Then she began to cringe, raising her head in a long drawn out canine howl, her arms stretched in front of her with the palms outwards.

With a roar they closed on her.

Faustaff began to run forward bent on trying to help the girl. Steifflomeis pulled at his arm.

'Too late,' he said. 'It never takes long.'

The group was already backing away. Faustaff glimpsed the mangled corpse of the girl lying on the ground, the dog-skin draped across her.

Bloody-mouthed, the horned man ran towards the fire and pulled a brand from it. Others brought wood that had already been gathered, heaping it around the girl. The wood was ignited and the pyre began to burn.

A wordless, ululating song began to come from the lips of the group and another dance began; this time it seemed to symbolise exaltation of some kind.

Faustaff turned away. 'That is nothing but magic, Steifflomeis—primitive superstition. What kind of perverse minds have your principals if they can produce scientific miracles and—permit *that*!'

'Permit? They encourage it. It is necessary to every simulation.'

'How can ritual sacrifice be necessary to a modern society?'

'You ask that, after your own simulation has just destroyed itself? There was little difference, you know—only the scale and the complexity. The woman died quickly. She might have died more slowly of radiation sickness on E-1 if that was where she came from.'

'But what purpose does a thing like that serve?'

Steifflomeis shrugged. 'Ah, purpose Faustaff. You think there is purpose?'

'I must think so, Steifflomeis.'

'It is supposed to serve a limited purpose, that sort of ritual. Even in your terms, it should be obvious that primitive peoples symbolise their fears and wishes in ritual. The cowardly dog, the malevolent woman—both were destroyed in that rite you witnessed.'

'Yet in reality, they continue to exist. That kind of ritual achieves nothing.'

'Only a temporary feeling of security. You are right. You are a rational man, Faustaff. I still fail to understand why you would not join forces with me—for I am also a rational man. You cling to primitive instincts, naïve ideals. You refuse to let your reason have full reign over you. Then you are shocked by what you have just seen. It is within the power of neither of us to change those people, but we could have taken advantage of their weaknesses and at least benefited ourselves.'

Faustaff could think of no reply, but he remained deeply unconvinced by Steifflomeis's argument. He shook his head slowly.

Steifflomeis made an impatient movement. 'Still? I had hoped that you would join me in defeat!' He laughed.

They left the park and walked along a street. On lawns, in the streets, on vacant lots and in gardens, the ritualistic revels of E-Zero were taking place. Steifflomeis and Faustaff were unnoticed and undisturbed. It was more than a reversion to the primitive,

Faustaff thought as they wandered through the scenes of dark carnival, it was a total adoption of the identities of psychological-mythical archetypes. As Steifflomeis had said, every man and woman had their rôle. These rôles fell into a few definite categories. The more outstanding ones dominated the rest. He saw men and women in cowled cloaks, their faces hidden, driving dozens of naked acolytes before them with flails or tree-branches; he saw a man copulating with a woman dressed as an ape, another woman, taking no part herself, seemed to be ordering an orgy. Everywhere were scenes of bloodshed and bestiality. It reminded Faustaff of the Roman Games, of the Dark Ages, of the Nazis. But there were other rituals that did not seem to fit in; they were quieter, less frenetic rituals that reminded Faustaff strongly of the few church services he had attended as a child.

Some kind of attitude was beginning to dawn in his confused mind, some realisation of why he had refused to agree with Steifflomeis in spite of everything he had discovered since their first meeting.

If he were witnessing magical ceremonies, then they were of two distinct kinds. He knew little about anthropology or superstition, mistrusted Jung and found mysticism boring—yet he had heard of Black Magic and White Magic, without understanding the differences that people claimed for them. Perhaps what had horrified him was the black variety. Were the other scenes he had noticed the manifestations of white magic?

The very idea of thinking in terms of magic or superstition appalled him. He was a scientist and to him magic meant ignorance and the encouragement of ignorance. It meant senseless murder, fatalism, suicide, hysteria. Suddenly the idea came to him that it also meant the Hydrogen Bomb and World War. It meant in short, the rejection of the human factor in one's nature—the total acceptance of the beast. But what was white magic? Ignorance, also probably. The black variety encouraged the bestial side of Man's nature, so perhaps the white variety encouraged—what?—the 'godly' side? The will to evil and the will to good. Nothing wrong with that as an idea. But Man was not a beast and he was not a god; he was Man. Intellect was what distinguished him from other species of animal. Magic, as far as Faustaff knew, rejected reason. Religion accepted it, of course, but hardly encouraged it. Only science accepted it and encouraged it. Faustaff suddenly saw mankind's social and psychological evolution in a clear, simple light. Science alone accepted Man as he was and sought to exploit his full potential.

Yet this planet he stood on was the creation of a superb understanding of science—and at the same time these dreadful magical rituals were allowed to take place.

For the first time Faustaff felt that the creators of the simulations had gone wrong somewhere—gone wrong in their own terms.

With a shock he acknowledged the possibility that not even they understood what they were doing.

He turned to suggest this to Steifflomeis, whom he had assumed was following just behind him.

But Steifflomeis had gone.

16

The Black Ritual

Then Faustaff glimpsed Steifflomeis just before the man turned a corner of the street. He began to run after him, pushing through the revellers who did not see him.

Steifflomeis was climbing into a car when Faustaff next saw him. Faustaff shouted but Steifflomeis did not reply. He started the car and was soon speeding away.

Another car was parked nearby. Faustaff climbed into it and gave chase.

More than once he was forced to swerve to avoid groups of people who were, like the others, completely oblivious of him, but he kept on Steifflomeis's trail without too much difficulty.

Steifflomeis was on the Long Beach road. Soon the sea was visible ahead. Steifflomeis began to follow the coast and Faustaff noticed that even the seashore was not free of its rituals. There was a big, old hacienda-style house visible ahead and Faustaff saw Steifflomeis turn his car into its drive.

Faustaff wasn't sure that Steifflomeis had realised he was being followed. Out of caution he stopped his own car a short distance before he reached the house. He got out and began to walk towards it.

By the time Faustaff had walked warily up the drive, he found Steifflomeis's car empty. Evidently the man had gone inside.

The front door of the house was locked. He walked around it until he came to a window. He looked in. The window opened into a large room that seemed to take up most of the ground floor.

Steifflomeis was in there and so were a great many others. Faustaff saw Maggy White there. She was glowering at Steifflomeis who wore his familiar mocking grin. Maggy White was dressed in a loose black robe. Its hood was thrown back over her shoulders. Apart from her, only Steifflomeis wore any kind of conventional clothing.

The others all wore black hoods and nothing else. The women knelt in the centre, their bowed heads towards Maggy White. The men stood around the walls. Some of them held large, black candles. One of them gripped a huge mediaeval sword.

Maggy White seated herself in a throne-like chair at one end of the room. She was speaking to Steifflomeis who gestured at her and left the room for a moment to reappear wearing a similar robe to the one she wore.

Maggy White disapproved but seemed to be able to do nothing to stop Steifflomeis.

Faustaff wondered why she should be involving herself in a ritual. It was, even to him, evidently a black magic ritual, with Maggy representing the Queen of Darkness or whatever it was. Steifflomeis now seated himself at the other end of the room and arranged his robe, smiling at Maggy and saying something which caused her to frown even more heavily.

From what he knew of such things, Faustaff supposed that Steifflomeis was representing the Prince of Darkness. He seemed to remember that the woman usually had a male lieutenant.

Two of the men went out and came back with a very beautiful young girl. She was certainly under twenty and probably much younger. She seemed totally dazed, but not in the same trancelike state as the others. Faustaff got the impression that she had not undergone the psychological reversal that the rest had suffered. Her blonde hair was piled on her head and her body looked as if it had been oiled.

The kneeling women rose as she entered and they stepped back towards the wall to line it like the men.

Rather reluctantly, Maggy signed to Steifflomeis who rose and walked jauntily towards the girl, parodying the ritualistic movements of the people. The two men forced the girl down so that she was lying on her back in front of Steifflomeis who stared smilingly down at her. He half-turned to Maggy and spoke. The woman pursed her lips and her eyes were angry.

To Faustaff it seemed that Maggy White might be going through with something she did not like, but doing it conscientiously. Steifflomeis, on the other hand, was enjoying himself, plainly taking a delight in his power over the others.

He knelt in front of the girl and began to caress her body. Faustaff saw the girl's head jerk suddenly and her eyes flare into awareness. He saw her begin to struggle. The two men stepped forward and held her.

Faustaff looked down and a saw a large flat stone, used as part of the garden's decoration. He picked it up and flung it through the window.

He had expected the people to be startled by his action, but as he clambered through the window he saw that only Maggy White and Steifflomeis were staring at him.

'Leave her alone, Steifflomeis,' Faustaff said.

'Someone has to do it, professor,' Steifflomeis said calmly. 'Besides which, we are the best people for the job, Miss White and myself. We do not act from any kind of instinct. There is no lust in us—is there, Miss White?'

Maggy White simply shook her head, her lips tight.

'We have no instincts whatsoever, professor,' Steifflomeis went on. 'It is a source of regret to Miss White, I think, but not to me. After all, you are an example of how certain instincts can be harmful to a man.'

'I've seen you angry and frightened,' Faustaff reminded him.

'Certainly I might have expressed anger and fear —but these were mental states, not emotional ones, or is there no difference in your terms, professor?'

'Why are you taking part in these things?' Faustaff ignored Steifflomeis's question and addressed them both.

'For amusement in my case,' Steifflomeis said. 'I am equipped to experience sensual pleasure, also—

though I do not spend a lifetime seeking it as you seem to.'

'There could be more to it,' Maggy White said quietly. 'I've already said this to you—maybe they can experience more pleasure.'

'I'm aware of your obsession, Miss White,' Steifflomeis smiled. 'But I am sure you're wrong. Everything they do is on a puny scale.' He looked at Faustaff. 'You see, professor, Miss White feels that by taking part in these rites it will somehow confirm on her a mysterious ecstacy. She thinks you have something we do not.'

'Perhaps we have,' Faustaff said.

'Perhaps it is not worth having,' Steifflomeis suggested.

'I'm not sure,' Faustaff looked at the people around him. The two men were still holding the girl, though now she seemed to have lapsed into a similar state to their own. 'It doesn't have to be this.'

'No indeed.' Steifflomeis's tone was sardonic. 'It could be something else. I think your friends Nancy Hunt and Gordon Ogg are involved in something you would prefer.'

'Are they all right?'

'Perfectly at this stage. They have come to no physical harm.' Steifflomeis grinned.

'Where are they?'

'They ought to be somewhere nearby.'

'Hollywood,' Maggy White said. 'One of the film company lots.'

'Which one?'

'Simone-Dane-Keene, I think. It's almost an hour's drive.'

163

Faustaff pushed the two men aside and picked up the girl.

'Where do you think you're taking her?' Steifflomeis mocked. 'She won't know anything after the activation.'

'Call me a dog in the manger,' Faustaff said as he carried the girl towards the front door and unlatched it.

He walked out to the street, reached his car, dumped the girl in the back seat and began the drive towards Hollywood.

17

The White Ritual

The car was fast and the freeways clear. As he drove, Faustaff wondered about the pair he had left. From what Steifflomeis had said, it was fairly obvious that they weren't human; were probably, as he'd suspected, near-human androids, more advanced versions of the robot D-squaders.

He hadn't asked the nature of the ritual in which, he assumed, Nancy and Gordon had become involved. He simply wanted to reach them as soon as possible so that he could be of help to them if they needed it.

He knew the S-D-K lot. S-D-K had been the biggest of the old-style motion picture makers on E-1. He had once visited the lot from curiosity on one of his occasional trips to E-1 Los Angeles.

Every so often he found it necessary to slow the car and steer through or around a throng of people performing what were to him obscure rites. They were not all obscene or violent, but the sight of the blank faces was sufficient to disturb him.

He had noticed a change, however. The buildings seemed in slightly sharper focus than when he had first arrived on E-Zero. The impression of newness, too, was beginning to wear off a little. Evidently these pre-activation rites had some link with the altering nature of the new planet. From his own experience he knew that it was this world's influence which produced the inability to associate properly, the quite rapid loss of personal identity, the slipback into the rôle of whatever psychological archetype was strongest in the particular psyche of the individual; but there also seemed to be a kind of feed-back where the people somehow helped to give the planet a more positive atmosphere of reality. Faustaff found the idea hard to grasp in any terms familiar to him.

He was nearing Hollywood now. He could see the big illuminated S-D-K sign ahead. Soon, he was turning into the lot. It was silent, apparently empty. He got out of the car, leaving the girl where she was. He locked the doors and began to walk in the direction of a notice which said *No. 1 STAGE.*

A door was set in the concrete wall. It was covered with cautionary signs. Faustaff pushed it open and looked inside. The jungle of cameras and electronic equipment partially hid a set. It looked like a set for an historical film. There was nobody in sight.

Faustaff tried the next stage. He walked in. There were no cameras about and all the equipment seemed neatly stowed. A set was up, however. It was probably being used for the same film. It showed the interior of a mediaeval castle. For a moment Faustaff wondered at the craftsmen who had built the set so that it looked so convincing.

There was a ritual being enacted on the set. Nancy Hunt was wearing a white, diaphanous shift and her red hair had been combed out and arranged to flow over her back and shoulders. Beside her was a man dressed in black armour that looked real. Either the costume was from the film, or else it had come from the same source as all the other costumes that Faustaff had seen. The man in black armour was drawing down his visor. He had a huge broadsword in his right hand.

With a measured tread another figure came clumping from the wings. It was Gordon Ogg, also in full armour of bright steel with a plain white surcoat over it. He held a large sword in his right hand.

Faustaff shouted: 'Nancy! Gordon! What are you doing?'

They didn't hear. Evidently they were as much in a dreamlike state as the rest.

With peculiar movements which resembled, to Faustaff, the highly mannered motions of a traditional Japanese mime-play, Ogg approached Nancy and the black-armoured man. His lips moved in speech, but Faustaff could tell that no words sounded.

In an equally formal way the black-armoured man gripped Nancy's arm and pulled her back, away from Ogg. Ogg now lowered his visor and seemed to challenge the other man with a movement of his sword.

Faustaff didn't think that Ogg was in any danger. He watched as Nancy stepped to one side and Ogg and his opponent touched swords. Shortly the black-armoured man dropped his sword and knelt in front of Gordon Ogg. Ogg then threw away his sword. The man rose and began to strip off his armour.

Nancy came forward and also knelt before Ogg. Then she got up and left the set, returning with a large golden cup which she offered to Ogg. He took it and drank from it—or pretended to, since Faustaff could see it was actually empty. Ogg picked up his sword and sheathed it.

Faustaff realised that he had only witnessed a small part of the ceremony and it now seemed over. What would Nancy and Gordon do?

There was a little more mime, with Nancy appearing to offer herself to Ogg and being sympathetically rejected. Then Ogg turned and began to move off the set, followed by everyone else. He held the golden cup high. It was obviously a symbol that meant something to him and the others.

Faustaff wondered if it represented the Holy Grail, and then wondered what the Holy Grail represented in Christian mythology and mysticism. Didn't it have a much older origin? Hadn't he read about a similar bowl appearing in Celtic mythology? He couldn't be sure.

Ogg, Nancy and the rest were now walking past him. He decided to follow them. At least he would be able to keep a watchful eye on his friends to make sure they didn't come to harm. It was, he reflected, like trying to deal with a somnambulist. It was probably even more dangerous to attempt to wake them up. Sleep-walkers, he now remembered, were said to perform rituals of this kind sometimes—usually simpler, but occasionally quite complex. There must surely be a link.

The procession left the set and walked out into the

arena-like compound. Tall concrete walls rose on every side.

They paused here and turned their faces to the sun, Gordon raising the bowl towards it, as if to catch its rays. A subdued chanting could now be heard coming from them all. It was a wordless chant —or at least in a language completely unfamiliar to Faustaff. It had vague affinities, with Greek, but it was more like the Voice of Tongues which Faustaff had heard on television once. How had it been described by a psychologist? The language of the unconscious. It was the kind of sound people used in their sleep sometimes, Faustaff found it slightly unnerving as he listened to the chant.

They were still chanting as Steifflomeis made his appearance. He had found a sword from somewhere and was gleefully leading the black-hooded acolytes into the arena. Maggy White, looking rather uncertain, followed behind. She seemed to be almost as much in Steifflomeis's power as the men who were with him.

Gordon Ogg turned as Steifflomeis shouted something in the same strange language they had been chanting in. From Steifflomeis the words seemed halting, as if he had learned them with difficulty.

Faustaff knew that Steifflomeis was shouting a challenge.

Gordon Ogg handed the cup to Nancy and drew his sword.

Watching the scene, Faustaff was suddenly struck by its ludicrousness. He began to laugh aloud. It was his old laugh, rich and warm, totally without tension. The laughter was picked up by the high walls and amplified, its echoes rolling around the arena.

For a moment everyone seemed to hear it and hesitated. Then, with a yell, Steifflomeis leapt at Ogg.

This action only caused Faustaff to laugh the more.

18

The Encounter

Steifflomeis seemed bent on killing Ogg, but he was such an inept swordsman that the Englishman, plainly trained in fencing, defended himself easily, in spite of the fact that his movements were so formal.

Faustaff snorted with laughter and stepped forward to grasp Steifflomeis's arm. The android was startled. Faustaff removed the sword from his hand.

'This is all part of the ritual!' Steifflomeis said seriously. 'You're breaking the rules again.'

'Calm down, Steifflomeis,' Faustaff chuckled and wiped his eyes. 'No need to get emotional.'

Gordon was still going through the motions of defence. He looked so much like Don Quixote in his armour and long moustache that his behaviour seemed funnier than ever to Faustaff who started to roar with laughter again.

Ogg began to look bewildered. His movements became more hesitant and less formal. Faustaff placed himself in front of him. Ogg blinked and lowered his sword. He frowned at Faustaff for a moment and then snapped down his visor and stood there rigidly, like a statue.

Faustaff raised his fist and tapped on the helmet. 'Come out of there, Gordon—you don't need the armour any more. Wake up, Gordon!'

He saw that the others were beginning to stir. He went up to Nancy and stroked her face. 'Nancy?'

She smiled vaguely, without looking at him.

'Nancy—it's Faustaff.'

'Faustaff,' she murmured distantly. 'Fusty?'

He grinned. 'The same.'

She looked up at him, still smiling. He chuckled and she looked into his eyes. Her smile broadened. 'Hi, Fusty. What's new?'

'You'd be surprised,' he said. 'Have you ever seen anything so funny?' He waved his hand to indicate the costumed figures about them. He pointed at the suit of armour. 'Gordon's in there,' he told her.

'I know,' she said. 'I really thought I was dreaming—you know, one of those dreams where you know you're dreaming but can't do anything about it. It was quite a nice dream.'

'Nothing wrong with dreams, I guess,' Faustaff said, putting his arm round her and hugging her. 'They serve their purpose, but . . .'

'This dream was serving a purpose until you interrupted it,' Maggy White said.

'But did you agree with the purpose?' Faustaff asked her.

'Well—yes. The whole thing is necessary. I told you.'

'I still don't know the original purposes for the simulations,' Faustaff admitted. 'But it seems to me that nothing can be achieved by this sort of thing.'

'I'm not sure,' Maggy White replied thoughtfully.

172

'I don't know . . . I'm still loyal to the principals, but I wonder . . . They don't seem very successful.'

'You're not kidding,' Faustaff agreed feelingly. 'What have they scrapped? A thousand simulations?'

'They'll never succeed,' Steifflomeis sneered. 'They've lost touch completely. Forget them.'

Maggy White turned on him angrily. 'This whole fiasco is your work, Steifflomeis. If you hadn't disobeyed your orders E-Zero would now be well on the way to normal activation. I don't know what's going to happen now. This will be the first time that anything has gone wrong *before* full activation!'

'You should have listened to me. We need never have allowed full activation if we had been careful. We could have ruled this world easily. We could have defied the principals. At best all they could have done would have been to start afresh.'

'There isn't time to start afresh. It would be tantamount to destroying their whole project, what you would have done!' Maggy glowered at him. 'You tried to defeat the principals!'

Steifflomeis turned his back on her with a sigh.

'You're too idealistic. Forget them. They are failures.'

Gordon Ogg's armour creaked. His arm moved towards his visor and slowly began to raise it. He looked out at them, blinking.

'By God,' he said wonderingly. 'Am I really dressed up in this stuff. I thought I was . . .'

'Dreaming? You must be hot in there, Gordon,' Faustaff said. 'Can you get it off?'

Ogg tugged at the helmet. 'I think it screws off,'

he said. Faustaff grasped the helmet and with some difficulty eased it round. Ogg took it off. They began to unstrap the rest of the armour, Nancy helping. A murmur of voices around them showed that both the people who had been with Steifflomeis and the people who had followed Gordon and Nancy were now waking up, confused.

Faustaff saw Maggy White stoop towards the sword and jumped up from where he was trying to unbuckle Gordon's left greave.

She had brought the sword down on Steifflomeis's skull before he could reach her. He turned towards her with a smile, reached out for her, and then toppled. The top of his head had caved in completely, showing the brain. No blood came. Maggy began to hack at his body until Faustaff stopped her. She became impassive, looking down at Steifflomeis's corpse. 'A work of art,' she said. 'Like me.'

'What are you going to do now?' Faustaff asked her.

'I don't know,' she said. 'Everything's gone wrong. All the rites you've seen are only the beginning. There's a series of huge assemblies later on— the final pre-activation rituals. You've broken the pattern.'

'Surely what's happened can't make much difference on a world scale.'

'You don't understand. Every symbol means something. Every individual has a rôle. It's all connected together. It's like a complicated electronic circuit—break it in one place and the whole thing seizes up. These rituals may seem horrifying and primitive to you—but they were inspired by a deeper knowledge of scientific principles than any-thing you're likely to have. The rituals establish the basic pattern of every individual's life. His inner drives are expressed and given form in the pre-acti-vation rituals. This means that when he "wakes up" and begins to lead his ordinary life, the code is im-printed in him and he will exist according to that code. Only a few, comparatively speaking, find new codes—new symbols—new lives. You're one of them—the most successful.

'Circumstances and your own integrity have en-abled you to do what you have done. What the result will be, I can't think. There seems to be no division between your inner life and your outer personality. It's as if you are playing a rôle whose influence goes beyond the bounds of the principals' experiments and affects them directly. I don't think they intend-ed to produce a type like you.'

'Will you tell me now who these "principals" are?' Faustaff asked her quietly.

'I can't,' she said. 'I obey them and I have been instructed to reveal as little about them as possible. Steifflomeis said far too much and by that action, among others, helped to create this situation. Per-haps we should have killed you straight away. We had a number of opportunities. But we were both curious and delayed things for too long. We were both, in our ways, fascinated by you. As you can see, we let your personality assume too much control over us.'

'We must do something,' Faustaff told her gently.

'I agree. Let's go back to the house first and talk it over.'

'What about all these others?'

'We can't do much for them—they're confused, but they'll be all right for a while.'

Outside the movie lot stood the small truck in which Steifflomeis had obviously brought his followers. Faustaff's car stood near it. In it a naked girl tugged at the doors and hammered on the window. Seeing them, she began to wind the window down.

'What the hell's going on?' she asked in a harsh, Brooklyn accent. 'Is this a kidnapping or something? Where am I?'

Faustaff unlocked the door and let her out.

'Jesus!' she said. 'What is it—a nudist camp? I want my clothes.'

Faustaff pointed back at the main gate of the lot. 'You'll find some in there,' he told her.

She looked up at the S-D-K sign. 'You're making a movie? Or is this one of those Hollywood parties I've heard about?'

Faustaff chuckled. 'With a figure like that you *ought* to be in pictures. Go and see if anyone spots you.'

She sniffed and began to walk towards the gate.

Gordon Ogg and Nancy got into the back seats and Maggy White climbed in beside Faustaff as he started the car, turned it neatly in the street and drove towards downtown L.A.

People were wandering about everywhere, many of them still in their ritual costumes. They looked puzzled and a bit dazed. They were arguing and talking among themselves. There didn't seem to be much trouble; nobody looked afraid. There were a few

176

cars on the road and sometimes a group of people would wave to him to stop as he passed, but he just waved back with a grin.

Everything seemed funny to him now. He realised that he was his old self again and wondered how and where he had started to lose his sense of humour.

Faustaff noticed, as he passed the spot, that the Time Dump had vanished and the anachronisms were gone, too. Everything looked fairly normal.

He asked Maggy White about it.

'Those things are automatically eradicated,' she told him. 'If they don't fit the pattern then the simulation can't work smoothly until everything is rationalised. The pre-activation process gets rid of anything like that. Since it's been interrupted, perhaps a few anachronisms will continue to exist. I don't know. It hasn't happened before on any large scale. It's like anything else, you see. The apparatus can't be tested thoroughly until it is tried out on whatever it was designed for. This is another function of the pre-activation process.'

The house, in which they'd travelled from E-3 to E-Zero, was still there and so was the cathedral, visible behind it.

Faustaff had a thought. He dropped the other three at the house and drove round to the cathedral. Even before he opened the door he heard shouting echoing around inside the building.

There was Orelli, still nailed to the cross. But he was far from tranquil. His face was twisted in pain.

'Faustaff!' he said hoarsely as the professor approached. 'What happened to me? What am I doing here?'

Faustaff found a candlestick that could probably be used to get the nails out.

'This is going to be painful, Orelli,' he said.

'Get me down. It couldn't be any more painful.'

Faustaff began to lever the nails from Orelli's flesh. He took the man in his arms and laid him on the altar. He moaned in agony.

'I'll get you back to the house,' Faustaff said, picking up the ex-cardinal. 'There'll probably be dressings of some kind there.'

Orelli was weeping as Faustaff carried him out to the car. Faustaff felt that it wasn't the pain that was making Orelli weep, it was probably the memory of the dream he had only recently awakened from.

Driving away from the cathedral, Faustaff decided that it would be better to go to the nearest hospital. Presumably it would be equipped with antibiotics and medicated gauze.

It took him a quarter of an hour to find a hospital. He went into its empty hall and through to the emergency rooms. In a big medical chest he found everything he wanted and began to treat Orelli.

By the time he had finished, the ex-cardinal was asleep from the sedative he had administered.

Faustaff took him to a bed and tucked him in.

Orelli would be all right for a while, he decided.

He drove back to the house, parked the car and went inside. Maggy White, Gordon Ogg and Nancy were sitting in the living-room, drinking coffee and eating sandwiches.

The scene seemed so normal as to be incongruous. Faustaff told them what he had done with Orelli and sat down to have some food and coffee.

178

As they finished and Faustaff lit cigarettes for himself and Nancy, Maggy White seemed to come to a decision.

'We could use the machinery in this house to get to the principals,' she said thoughtfully. 'Would you like me to take you to them, Faustaff?'

'Wouldn't that be going against your instructions?'

'It is the best thing I can think of. I can't do anything else now.'

'Naturally I'd like to contact your principals,' Faustaff nodded. He now began to feel excited. 'Though at this stage I can't see any way of sorting out the mess that everything's in. Do you know how many of the other simulations still exist?'

'No. Perhaps they have all been destroyed by now.'

Faustaff sighed. 'Their efforts and mine both appear to have been wasted.'

'I'm not sure,' she said. 'Let's see. We'd have to leave your friends behind.'

'Do you mind?' Faustaff asked them. They shook their heads. 'Perhaps you could go and make sure Orelli's all right,' Faustaff suggested. He told them where the hospital was. 'I know how we all felt towards him, but he's paid a big enough price, I think. I don't think you'll hate him when you see him. I'm not sure his sanity will survive even now.'

'Okay,' Nancy said, getting up. 'I hope you'll get back soon, Fusty. I want to see more of you.'

'It's mutual,' he smiled. 'Don't worry. Goodbye, Gordon.' He shook hands with Ogg. 'See you!'

They left the house.

179

Faustaff followed Maggy White into the other room where the equipment was.

'There's just one button to press,' she told him. 'But it only works for Steifflomeis or me. I'd have used it before if I could have got the house to myself, but I got diverted—I had to stay to see what you did.' She reached out and pressed the button.

The walls of the house seemed to change colour, rapidly going through the whole spectrum; they seemed to flow in on Faustaff, covering him with soft light, then they flattened out.

They stood on a vast plateau roofed by a huge, dark dome. Light came from all sides, the colours merging to become a white that was not really white, but a visible combination of all colours.

And giants looked down on them. They were human, with calm, ascetic features, completely naked and hairless. They were seated in simple chairs that did not appear to have any real substance and yet supported them perfectly.

They were about thirty feet high, Faustaff judged.

'My principals,' Maggy White said.

'I'm glad to meet you at last,' Faustaff told them. 'You seem to be in some sort of dilemma.'

'Why have you come here?' One of the giants spoke. His voice did not seem in proportion to his size. It was quiet and well-modulated, without emotion.

'To make a complaint, among other things,' said Faustaff. He felt that he should be overawed by the giants, but perhaps all the experiences that had led up to this meeting had destroyed any sense of wonder he might have had otherwise. And he felt the giants had bungled too much to deserve a great deal of respect from him.

Maggy White was explaining everything that had happened. When she finished, the giants got up and walked through the walls of light. Faustaff sat down on the floor. It felt hard and cold and it made the parts of his body that touched it feel as if they had received a slight local anaesthetic. Its perpetual changing of colour didn't help him to feel any more comfortable.

'Where have they gone?' he asked Maggy.

'To debate what I have told them,' she said. 'They shouldn't be long.'

'Are you ready to tell me who they actually are?'

'Let them tell you,' she said. 'I'm sure they will.'

19

Conversation with the Principals

The principals soon returned. When they had seated themselves one of them spoke.

'There is a pattern to everything,' he said. 'But everything makes the pattern. The human failing is to make patterns out of parts of the whole and call it the whole. Time and Space has a pattern, but you see only a few elements on your simulations. Our science reveals the full dimensions and enables us to create the simulations.'

'I understand that,' said Faustaff. 'But why do you create the simulations in the first place.'

'Our ancestors evolved on the original planet many millions of years ago. When their society had developed to the necessary point, they set off to explore the universe and understand it. Approximately ten thousand of your years ago we returned to the planet of our origin, having mapped and studied the universe and learned all its fundamental principles. We found that the society that had produced us had decayed. We expected that of course. But what we had scarcely realised was the extent to which we ourselves had been physically changed by our journeyings. We are immortals, in the sense that we shall exist until the end of the current phase of the universe. This knowledge has altered our psychology, naturally. In your terms we have become superhuman but we feel this as a loss rather than an accomplishment. We decided to attempt to reproduce the civilisation that had produced us.

'There were a few primitive inhabitants left on the Earth, which had long-since begun a metamorphosis into an altered chemical state. We revitalised the planet, giving it an identical nature to the one it had had when civilisation first began to exist in any real form. We expected the inhabitants to react to this. We expected—and there was no cause then to expect otherwise—to develop a race which would rapidly achieve an identical civilisation to the one which had created us. But the first experiment failed —the inhabitants stayed on the same level of barbarism that they had been on when we first found them, but they began to fight one another. We decided to create an entirely new planet and try again. So as not to alter the balance of the universe, we extended a kind of "well" into what you call, I believe, "subspace", and built our new planet there. This proved a failure, but we learnt from it. Since then we have built more than a thousand simulations of the original Earth and have gradually been adding to our understanding of the complexity of the project we undertook. Everything on every planet has a part to play. A building, a tree, an animal, a man. All link in as essentials to the structure. They have a physical rôle to play in the ecological and sociological nature of the planet, and they have a psychological rôle—a symbolic nature. That is why we find it useful to have the populace of every new simulation (which is drawn from previous abandoned simulations) externalise and dramatise its symbolic and psychological rôle before full activation. To some extent it is also therapeutic and in many ways has the effect of simulating the birth and childhood of the adults we use. You doubtless noticed that there were no children on the new simulation. We find children very difficult to use on a freshly activated world.'

'But why all those simulations?' Faustaff said. 'Why not one planet which you could—judging by what you do anyway—brainwash *en masse* and channel it the way you want to.'

'We are trying to produce an identical evolutionary pattern to the one which produced us. It would be impractical to do as you suggest. The psychological accretions would build-up too rapidly. We need a fresh environment every time. All this was considered before we began work on the first simulation.'

'And why don't you interfere directly with the worlds? Surely you could destroy them as easily as you create them.'

'They are not easily created and are not easily destroyed. We dare not let a hint of our presence get to the simulations. We did not exist when our ancestors evolved, therefore no-one should guess we exist now. We use our androids for destroying the failed simulations, or, for more sophisticated work, we use near-humans like the one who brought you here. They seem to be human and the natural assumption, if their activities are discovered and their missions fail, is that they are employed by other human beings. It is a very delicate kind of experiment, since it involves complicated entities like yourself, and we cannot afford, normally, to interfere directly. We do not want to become gods. Religion has a function in a society's earliest stages, but that function is soon replaced by the sciences. To provide what would be to your people "proof" of supernatural beings would be completely against our interest.'

'What of the people you kill? Have you no moral attitude to that?'

'We kill very few. Normally the population of one simulation is transferred to another. Only the children are destroyed in any quantity.'

'*Only* the children!'

'I understand your horror. I understand your feelings towards children. It is necessary that you should have them—it is a virtue when you have these feelings in any strength—in your terms. In our terms, the whole race is our children. Compare our destruction of your immature offspring to your own destruction of male sperm and female ovum in preventing birth. Your feelings are valid. We have no use for such feelings. Therefore, to us they are invalid.'

Faustaff nodded. 'I can see that. But I *have* these feelings. Besides which, I think there is a flaw in your argument. We feel that it is wrong to expect our children to develop as duplicates of ourselves. This defeats progress in any sense.'

'We are not seeking progress. There is no progress to be made. We know the fundamental principles of everything. We are immortal, we are secure.'

Faustaff frowned for a moment and then asked, 'What are your pleasures?'

'Pleasures?'

'What makes you laugh, for instance?'

'We do not laugh. We would know joy—fulfilment—if our experiment were to be successful.'

'So, currently, you have no pleasures. Nothing sensual or intellectual?'

'Nothing.'

'Then you are dead, in my terms,' Faustaff said. 'Forget about the simulations. Can't you see that all your energies have been diverted into a ridiculous, useless experiment? Let us develop as we will—or destroy ourselves if we must. Let me take the knowledge you have given me back to E-Zero and tell everyone of your existence. You have kept them in fear, you have allowed them to despair, you have, in certain directions, kept them in ignorance. Turn your attention to yourselves—look for pleasure, create things to give you pleasure. Perhaps in time you would succeed in reproducing this Golden Age you speak of—but I doubt it. Even if you did, it would be a meaningless achievement, particularly if the eventual result was a race like yourselves. You have logic. Use it to find enjoyment in subjective pursuits. A thing does not have to have meaning to be enjoyed. Where are your arts, your amusements, your entertainments?'

'We have none. We have no use for them.'

'Find a use.'

The giant rose. His companions got up at the same time.

Once again they left the place and Faustaff waited, assuming they were debating what he had said.

They returned eventually.

'There is a possibility that you have helped us,' said the giant as he and his companions seated themselves.

'Will you agree to let E-Zero develop without interference?' Faustaff asked.

'Yes. And we shall allow the remaining subspacial simulations to exist. There is one condition.'

'What's that?'

'Our first illogical act—our first—joke—will be to have all the thirteen remaining simulations existing together in ordinary space-time. What influence this will in time have on the structure of the universe we cannot guess, but it will bring an element of uncertainty into our lives and thus will help us in our quest for pleasures. We shall have to enlarge your sun and replace the other planets in your system, for the thirteen worlds will constitute a much larger mass since we visualise them as being close together and easily accessible to one another. We feel that we shall be creating something that has no great practical use, within the limited sense of the word, but which will be pleasing and unusual to the eye. It will be the first thing of its kind in the universe.'

'You certainly work fast,' Faustaff smiled. 'I'm looking forward to the result.'

'No physical danger will result from what we do. It will be—spectacular, we feel.'

'So it's over—you're abandoning the experiment

187

altogether. I didn't think you'd be so easily convinced.'

'You have released something in us. We are proud of you. By accident we helped create you. We are not abandoning the experiment, strictly speaking. We are going to let it run its own course from now on. Thank you.'

'And thank you, gentlemen. How do I get back?'

'We will return you to E-Zero by the usual method.'

'What about Maggy White?' Faustaff said, turning towards the girl.

'She will stay with us. She might be able to help us.'

'Goodbye, then, Maggy,' Faustaff kissed her on the cheek and squeezed her arm.

'Goodbye,' she smiled.

The walls of light began to flow inwards, enfolding Faustaff. Soon they took on the shape of the room in the house.

He was back on E-Zero. The only difference was that the equipment had vanished. The room looked completely normal.

He went to the front door Gordon Ogg and Nancy were coming up the path.

'Good news,' he grinned, walking towards them. 'I'll tell you all about it. We've got a lot of work to do to help everybody organise themselves.'

20

The Golden Bridges

By the time the principals were ready to create their 'joke', the populations of the subspacial worlds had been informed of everything Faustaff could tell them. He had been interviewed for the press, given television and radio time, and there had been no questioning voices. Somehow, all he said struck the worlds' populations as being true. It explained what they saw around them, what they felt within them.

The time came, and everyone was ready for it, when the thirteen planets began to phase in to ordinary space-time.

Faustaff and Nancy were back in Los Angeles when it happened, standing in the garden of the house which had first brought them to E-Zero and where they now lived. It was night when the twelve other simulations made their appearance. The dark sky seemed to ripple gently and they were there; a cluster of worlds moving in unison through space, with E-Zero in the centre, like so many gigantic moons.

Faustaff recognised the green jungle world of E-12; the desert-sea world of E-3. There was the vast continental atoll that was the only land area on E-7;

the more normal-seeming worlds of E-2 and E-4; the mountainous world of E-11.

Now Faustaff received the impression that the sky was *flowing* and he realised that, miraculously the atmospheres of the Earth-simulations were merging to form a complete envelope around the world-cluster. Now the jungle world could supply oxygen to the worlds with less vegetation, and moisture would come from the worlds predominantly of water.

He saw E-1, as he craned his neck to see them all. It seemed covered by black and scarlet clouds. It was right, he felt, that it should have been included; a symbol of ignorance and fear, a symbol of what the idea of hell actually meant in physical terms. The atmosphere did not seem to extend to E-1, for though its presence was necessary, it had been isolated.

Faustaff realised that though the principals had made a joke, it was a joke with many points to it.

'I hope they don't get too earnest about this now,' Nancy said, hugging Faustaff's arm.

'I don't think they're going to be earnest for long,' he smiled. 'Just serious maybe. A good joke needs a spot of everything.' He shook his head in wonderment. 'Look at it all. It's impossible in our scientific terms, but they've done it. I've got to hand it to them; when they decide to be illogical, they go the whole hog!'

Nancy pointed into the sky. 'Look,' she said. 'What's happening now?'

There was a further movement in the sky. Other objects began to appear; great golden structures whose reflected light turned the night to near-day; arcs of flame, bridges of light between the worlds. Faustaff shielded his eyes to peer at them. They ran from world to world, spanning the distances like fiery rainbows. Only E-1 was not touched by them.

'That's what they are,' Faustaff said in realisation. 'They're bridges—bridges that we can cross to reach the other simulations. See . . .' he pointed to an object that hung in the sky above their heads, rapidly passing as the world turned on its axis—'there's one end of ours. We could reach it in a plane, then we could walk across, if we had a lifetime to spare! But we can build transport that will cross the bridges in a few days! These worlds are like islands in the same lake, and those bridges link us all together.'

'They're very beautiful,' said Nancy quietly.

'Aren't they!'

Faustaff laughed in pleasure at the sight and Nancy joined in.

They were still laughing when the sun rose, a massive, splendid sun that made Faustaff realise that he had never really known daylight until that moment.

The giant sun's rays caught the gold of the bridges so that they flamed even more brilliantly.

Used now to the code in which the principals had tried to write the history of his race, Faustaff looked at the bridges and understood the many things they meant; to him, to the worlds and to the men, women and children who must now all be looking up at them.

And in its isolation, E-1 glared luridly in the new daylight.

Faustaff and Nancy turned to look at it. 'There's

no need to fear that now, Nancy,' he said to her. 'We can start getting somewhere at last, as long as we remember to relax a bit. Those bridges mean understanding; communication . . .'

Nancy nodded seriously. Then she looked up at Faustaff and her expression turned into a spreading grin. She winked at him. He grinned and winked back.

They went into the house and were soon rolling about in bed together.

If you would like a complete list of Arrow books please send a postcard to
P.O. Box 29, Douglas, Isle of Man, Great Britain.